Winner of the Drue Heinz Literature Prize 1981

The Death of Descartes

The Death of Descartes

DAVID BOSWORTH

University of Pittsburgh Press

129404

for Jacquie

Published by the University of Pittsburgh Press, Pittsburgh, Pa. 15260
Copyright © 1981, David Bosworth
All rights reserved
Feffer and Simons, Inc., London
Manufactured in the United States of America
Second printing, 1982

Library of Congress Cataloging in Publication Data
Bosworth, David, 1947-
    The death of Descartes.

    I. Title.
PS3552.0813D4   813'.54   81-50637
ISBN 0-8229-3448-5   AACR2

"Excerpts from a Report of the Commission," copyright 1977 by The Antioch Review, Inc., first appeared in *The Antioch Review*, vol. 35, no. 2–3 (Spring–Summer 1977), and is reprinted by permission of the editors. "Psalm" first appeared in *Ploughshares*. "The Death of Descartes" first appeared in *The Agni Review*.

I would like to thank the National Endowment for the Arts for a fellowship grant which allowed me to complete a portion of this book. Special thanks to Sharon Dunn and Nolan Miller for their support.

Contents

Excerpts from a
Report of the Commission

*I*T IS THE SUMMER OF '65, THE LIP OF THE Apocalypse, on the cusp without knowing it, and you have not left me. Skirts are rising everywhere, stage curtains to the mysterious, hints of thigh and lower necklines, the Pill invented. The world winks, poised with promises, a *Playboy* centerfold beckoning to a high school graduate unaware of Sexual Politics and Primal Therapy, who practices instead, on the back seat of an old Corvair at the local drive-in movie theater, a simpler ideology. "No." "Yes." "*No.*" "*Yes.*" —is the only dialectic I know; and the only time that stops is the dashboard's broken clock; home late, arguing with parents, breath mints hastily chewed to mask the Smirnoff's and orange juice.

It is the summer of '65 and the Beach Boys are my oracle; theirs is a difficult message to follow, though, in landlocked Pennsylvania—no waves to ride, no T.M. yet to pacify, the Maharishi still in India. It's summer, but my father still must ride the 8:10 train to Philadelphia, still responds with a delicate sneer to my mother's well-intentioned pieties, to the Surgeon General and the New Frontier. He pretends to be broken in, worn and comfortable like the leather strap he clings to as the train shimmies through suburbia, but there are secrets in his eyes—heresies, bacchanalia. And Eddie Carlson, he rides too, but in his car, a souped-up Pontiac Firebird, a teased-haired

3

girlfriend beneath his arm. Best friends in grammar school, we don't do much together any more, but haven't yet been made aware that class oppression is our separator; and unemployed, Eddie waits, patches of rubber to mark each day, for greetings from the U.S. government.

Because it's the summer of '65, summer of guns and butter, of college boom and color television, body counts instead of lottery numbers; and you have not left me. We haven't even met. The parish paragon, you are saving yourself in some small town outside of Buffalo, consciousness unraised, a fanatic worshipper of Kennedys, polishing the gem of your virginity, dressed in a Catholic school uniform, your knees not showing. Meanwhile, tourists by the car and busful, carefully avoiding the surrounding ghettos, unaware though of their racism, solemnly march like Canterbury pilgrims through the cemetery at Arlington and bow before an eternal flame memorial.

A good year, '65, summer's fruition for the welcome-home babies of the World War II generation; coming of age, losing our virginity, sleep-walking our way into anarchy. Life's a beach party, a Pepsi commercial, a home movie of the holidays with clowning children and flinching mothers, caught by surprise in their hair curlers. Who would have guessed? Who then, replaying the film, frame by frame, backward and forward, could have discerned the evidence: the reticular plots, the rampant evil, cancer's seed cells, love already doomed before the lovers have even met? Who could have seen, in that vague shadow on the window's ledge, the murderous intent of an assassin's rifle?

Exhibit 2b-324: a child's worn catcher's mitt. Its thumb is split, its leather dried and cracked, the inside rotted from sweat, its Del Crandall signature barely legible as though the abraded inscription on an ancient statue. To the best of my recollection, I receive Exhibit 2b-324 when I'm eleven years old, on a Saturday afternoon in the spring of '59, spring of Little League and presidential primaries, Joe Kennedy out following the hustings, buying his son the nomination. My father buys me a catcher's mitt and, while taking a break from raking our lawn, presents it to me. He is his eyes that afternoon, no flickering sneers, no resigned cynicism, animated and intense, a keeper of mysteries. He cradles the glove in his hands as if it were some family totem or a royal diadem on a satin pillow whose transfer requires this special ritual, fatherly advice for the heir apparent. He smiles—a small, knowing, wonderful smile—unaware that his gift is a sexist one, unaware that he is oppressing me with this age-old macho knowledge he brings: how to break a glove in by rubbing it again and again, pausing to take in the commingled, exquisite scent of calfskin and linseed oil; how to admire a thing well-made, not just with your eyes but with your hands, your fingertips, the feel and flex, the sensual caress of softened leather.

He is his eyes that afternoon; the years of silence have been broken through. We sit together on the back steps, immense cumulus clouds passing overhead; our raked piles of splintered twigs, of dead grass and cracked leaves, lay abandoned, spring's ritual of readying the lawn delayed for a moment. For not yet aware of the fascist character of American sport, we, my father and I, are discussing the intricacies of the foul tip, of picking runners off second base, how to dig a curve out of the dirt, all the lore and craftsmanship of catching a baseball game. And when we're finished and the time has come to transfer the glove from father to son, he holds Exhibit 2b-324 above my hands, and pausing, gives me his final words, both a benediction and a warning, a standard of truth and an invocation of responsibility:

"You have to take care of a glove like this."

Theory 4a: "The Blueblood, Banker, Think Tank, Media, and Mantra Conspiracy." There exists a group, a certain wealthy and influential set of individuals, primarily but not exclusively American, who have been placed by insidious design in sensitive positions throughout society, certain key positions whose power when haphazardly applied would be benign, but when coordinated by a centralized, secret, and self-serving organization, becomes the single predominant force in the country and, therefore, the world. This group, The Group, which includes among its members some of the most prominent families in America (I need only mention the Rockefellers), deliberately plants its followers and their fellow travelers within the intelligensia and the media, and through their consequent manipulation of public opinion, through *the planned obsolescence of popular values and philosophies,* creates an endless series of new markets for their corporations.

Incense, herbal tea, natural food packaging, radical posters, men's hair salons, Far Eastern religious textbooks and icons—who do you think, behind all the middlemen and holding companies, actually controls these new goods and services? Who do you think has cleverly cornered the spiritual commodities market? It's this group, The Group; they're the ones who hire opinion-shapers and import gurus from India in order to instigate these new social and religious movements; they're the ones who promote disruptive philosophical notions, breaking up our marriages; who support the sale of poisonous products, giving cancer to our fathers; who start the wars, killing our best friends from grammar school; and all so we'll be lonely and frightened and caught up in a crisis of belief and therefore vulnerable to these new movements and their attendant line of goods and services. Who do you think—their warehouses already stocked with

6

potentially profitable, black-rimmed photographs and bronze bust paperweights—sent Lee Harvey Oswald up to that sixth-floor window?

It's the fall of '67 and we count our education by the number of assumed truths we've rejected, by the lies we've inherited. Skirts have come off, replaced by faded jeans; fraternity pins by lace and beads; grass is in, but surreptitiously, politicians not aware that *their* sons and daughters are smoking it. It's fall, but with a son in college, my father still must ride that 8:10 train to Philadelphia, still hides those secrets in his eyes while pretending to blend in with briefcase-toting Republicans. A vast silence begins to descend, my father's version of the generation gap. He has nothing to say when I come home for the holidays; doesn't respond to my outraged challenges, to my uncut hair and downy moustache; instead, smiling sadly, chain-smokes pack after pack of Viceroy cigarettes. Meanwhile, Eddie Carlson is home on leave before they ship him overseas. Back straight, head shaved, able to kill in ten different ways, he is a man now and walks around town with a curious dignity, as if he'd been given the gift of prophecy, as if like my father, he's been told the secrets.

Because it's the fall of '67, fall of Lyndon Johnson and Robert MacNamara, of Jimi Hendrix and Owsley acid, head shops springing up everywhere, Peace and Love in Haight-Ashbury; and you have not left me. We haven't even made love. I circle you like a medieval castle, the forbidding guard of your Catholicism, its insulating moat and walls, the rack of conscience in its torture tower. No longer the parish paragon, you are still saving yourself, but for what, for whom, you do not know. The belief is gone, but the guilt remains—guilt, fear, and a wallet photo of J.F.K. I storm, retreat, use Trojan horse

7

strategies; attack with pleadings, reason—unaware, though, that I'm oppressing you, unaware that desire is bad karma, illusory and unsatisfying.

Because it's the fall of '67 and skirts barely cover pubic hair, the frontier of the New Morality; because virginity has become reactionary, and we have access to a mountain cabin. It is, to the best of my recollection, a perfect night, crisp and star-bright; grass is smoked, a long walk taken, hot chocolate sipped before an open fire; then to the bedroom arm in arm, clothes shed slowly, shyly but without alarm. I'm calmer, less pressing, and moving slowly, you don't resist me, my desire so pure, so focused that it seems almost meditative, this moment I've been waiting for. Pulling the covers back, stripping away the medieval restraints, I pause for a moment to take you in; and to the best of my recollection, I love you then as I have never loved before and never will again, awe-struck by your naked-ness. But I've been taught the fine art of admiring the beautiful; been shown the responsibilities attendant to it, and I say to myself as a reminder, a pledge: You have to take care of a woman like this . . . respect her, cherish her. And later, you lie beside me silently for a moment, distant, so distant, hair sprayed across the pillow, your lips moving soundlessly as if praying for atonement. Then you begin to cry, but quietly, to grieve this loss with dignity, death to a certain kind of idealism, your childhood shed on the sheets. Watching you, I reach out, moved to tears myself, and with my arms around you, whisper again and again like the counted phrases of a rosary penance: "It's all right—I won't hurt you. It's all right—I won't hurt you."

Do you remember the scene? Do you remember that fall of '67? The quilt-covered bed, the luxuriant spray of your auburn hair, my soft voice pressed against your ear above an embroi-

8

dered, tear-stained pillowcase? Would you have cried then if you had been shown the evidence, if you had seen the later headlines on the rancid gossip sheets? Would you have waited all those years outside of Buffalo, knees locked beneath school uniforms, if you had thought, as you do now, that in the back bedrooms of the White House, your Saint Jack was balling gangster molls? And would I have bothered to comfort you, would I have ever spent all that time laying siege on your virginity if I had thought, as I do now, that Libras are incompatible with Scorpios?

Exhibits 3c-42, 43: two black-and-white photographs. Both old, both creased, both posed pictures of groups of people; but there the similarities end. One, the larger, is of children, boys and girls, in loose rows, smiling or shy as the case may be according to their on-camera personalities; the other of men in uniform, heads shaved and backs stiff, rows straight, not a smile to be found on any face. One a picture of my fourth-grade class, the other a photo of an army platoon. Only with a second, closer look, with a kind of photographic analysis, can the true connection be seen, the one face that's duplicated: in the back row of both pictures, Eddie Carlson's pallid visage.

In fourth grade, I see Eddie every day, best friends who play together; after he's drafted, we meet only once, and then by accident at a local bar, both of us home for the holidays. Ours is an uneasy reunion; army khakis versus campus denim, army crew cut versus pony tail, we sip beer across a formica-top table like enemy soldiers in neutral territory. I slump, embarrassed and a bit guilty; Eddie sits up straight, detached, ironic. The army's changed him: he's quieter now and has acquired a strange half-smile that reminds me of my father's, full of secrets, private humor. Eyes averted, we drink our beers, occasionally moved by shared memories: hey, remember the time we stole the ballpoint pens, the times we snuck into the reservoir, the endless touch football games, two on two, the Weinberg twins against me and you; remember how we'd practice our plays well past dusk, me trying to catch your passes in the dark; how we learned each other's every move, the best pass combination in the grammar school . . . ?

But nostalgia can only carry us so far, the silence growing longer and longer, until we're eventually forced to turn to the war, the war Eddie will be fighting shortly. Even then, though, Eddie doesn't change; even then he retains his strange new aura of stoicism, reporting to me the date of his departure as matter-of-factly as a secretary confirming a business appointment. Amazed by him, I blurt out finally:

"But aren't you scared? Aren't you frightened at all?"

Eddie watches me silently for a moment, watches me in the same way my father does when I'm arguing a point at the dinner table—from a distance, from a different dimension, like some enlightened one who is sadly noting my ignorance. Then, without saying a word, he reaches into his pocket and hands me that black-and-white photograph of his army platoon.

"We had this sergeant," Eddie eventually says, lost in the story before it begins. "The biggest asshole I ever met. Sgt. Garth was his name and any one of us would've cut his balls off if we'd had the chance. He's the one who trained us for combat; he's the one who told us, grinning from ear to ear, that they were definitely shipping us over to Nam. It was just a minute or two before this picture was snapped—he said he was telling us then to make certain we'd be smiling for the photograph. And then, while we waited at attention, just having heard that we were heading for combat, he decided it was time to play a little game with us. Walking back and forth in front of the platoon, he pointed to each of us one by one, and like some love-sick girl plucking on a flower, called out loud his singsong predictions:

" 'You'll come back on your feet. . . . You'll come back in a box. . . . You, on your feet. . . . You, in a box. . . . On your feet. . . . In a box. . . . On your feet. . . . In a box. . . . On your feet. . . .' "

Eddie hesitates; his finger, which has been stabbing the air as he imitates the sergeant's game, points at me suddenly.

"In a box."

I wait, pinioned by his finger, arrow of fate; a long moment passes before Eddie's arm droops, before freed from the story's spell, he sips from his beer and nods his head.

"So you see, there's no reason for me to be scared. 'Cause I'm charmed, one of the lucky ones; 'cause Sergeant Garth guaranteed that I'll be coming back on my feet."

Eddie pauses and, glancing at me, that strange half-smile flickers across his features—the key, the qualifier to all that he means. Nodding to me, he twirls his beer between his fingertips:

"And you can always believe what an officer tells you."

There's a pause. I wait, but we're no longer occupying the same space, Eddie Carlson fading away, propelled inward by his half-smile, by his sad and private ironies. And that's when I first make the connection, when I first remember our old class picture . . . fourth-graders then, a team of best friends, quarterback and end, all those nights well past dusk, practicing to beat the Weinberg twins; I could catch his passes on faith, *on faith* in the dark, I knew his moves so well—perfect timing on a down-and-out. But could someone then have foreseen, studying our class photo with the latest techniques, the splitting up of that perfect team, the separate ways we all

11

would drift, the boys and girls of Miss Jensen's class? Could someone have foretold, marching before us like Sgt. Garth, what for each fourth-grader the future would.hold? Or predicted this reunion, its silences and separation, Eddie with his head shaved, drifting away on his island of irony, his resigned dignity, drifting away as though he were already heading for Southeast Asia; knowing the secrets, smiling at them, but not able, not permitted, to reveal them to me?

Theory 8e: "The Avenging Angel or Lone Gunman." There exists a single individual who is following me—perhaps some retired member of the C.I.A., a Cold War cowboy on a personal rampage; perhaps just some small-town loser bent on revenge—but in any case a single man, no co-conspirators, no ultimate motive beyond his own pathology. Although his identity remains elusive, this single man's biography will fit a predetermined pattern: deprived childhood, weak or absent father figure, poor academic record but not a discipline problem, generally inept in social relations, very probably afflicted with sexual dysfunction. Those few who do remember him at all will describe him as a shy man who wouldn't hurt·a fly, who minded his business and paid his rent on time; but beneath that innocuous and reserved exterior boils a cauldron of resentment and psychotic anger, a man trying to cope with a lifetime of failure.

Perhaps he's someone I've known all my life, a classmate I taunted in seventh grade, a war veteran who resents my draft evasion; perhaps it's a case of mistaken identity or a simple irrational hatred of my being. But whatever the case, he, this single man, this lone gunman, has latched onto me as the psychotic projection of his own inadequacies, as the secret cause of all his failures. And he follows me now, year in year

out, an avenging angel grown thin on his own malevolence,
killing my father, my friends, all the people and ideas that I
want to believe in; an unseen sniper who pumps bullet after
bullet into the corpse of my happiness.

It is the summer of '70, the pit of the Apocalypse, bottomed
out without knowing it; and you have not left me. Everyone
has died or been assassinated; Dr. King, Sharon Tate and Ho
Chi Minh, Czech democracy, the Lyndon Johnson presi-
dency, heir-apparent Bobby Kennedy—another bullet in the
corpse of your idealism; more nationally televised funerals
with zoom close-ups of grieving widows. Despite the sergeant's
guarantee, despite Richard Nixon's secret plan, Eddie Carlson
has not come home from the war—neither on his feet nor in
a box; has become instead an ambiguous acronym, an M.I.A.
in perpetual suspension. Disappointments add up; protests
change nothing; Chappaquiddick now a household word, there's
no one left we can trust anymore.

Because it's the summer of '70, the country's last fling at
radicalism, the old decade fading away, the Beatles splitting
up while Arab oil sheiks get their game together; and we're
not yet aware that radical chic will become passé, that law
schools will absorb the revolutionaries. Son and daughter of a
liberated age, showing solidarity with the poor of the city, we
decide to move in together, taking a two-room apartment in a
slum near campus. I hawk papers and volunteer time at a
welfare agency; you finish school and protest the Cambodia
invasion. Dishes pile up; money is short; sex begins to lose its
allure between housework squabbles and cockroach wars. On
a day in July, I come home to find you sitting on the bedroom
floor before a tilting pile of record albums; silent, eyes red,
strands of dampened hair clinging to your cheeks, you toy

13

with the black arm band you've worn since the Kent State killings on May the fourth. The first thought that enters my head as I rush toward you, panicking, is that someone's been assassinated.

"What's the matter? What's happened?"

You look up, body slumped, and say in an oddly distracted voice, "Haven't you noticed yet?"

You gestured vaguely, limp with resignation. I scan the room quickly—the rumpled bed, piles of dirty clothes, sunlight streaming through our soot-smeared window. Then, finally, I notice it, not what's there but what's missing, our one and only valued possession.

"The stereo? . . . Ripped off?" I pause, but you don't have to answer the obvious. "But how did they . . . ?" I turn around, about to check the door.

"Don't bother—I let them in."

"You *let* them in?"

"Oh yeah," you say, your features coming alive with sarcasm, "they were brothers—you know, fellow long-hairs, sons of the Revolution; hitched all the way from Philly for tomorrow's demonstration. And Sister Sucker here offered them a place to crash. But then I had to pick up some posters from Shelly, left the *brothers* alone for fifteen minutes . . ." You pause, tears filling your eyes one more time; picking up a record, you smash it on the floor. "Bastards!"

"Hey, it's all right; we can . . ."

But you brush away my comforting hand, still prefer your castle walls. Recovering by yourself, drying your eyes with the sleeve of your blouse, you say suddenly: "You know Billy Raskind?"

"Jan's old boyfriend? What's he got to do with . . ."

"He's hooked on smack."

14

I blink at you, confused; you're not making sense, in shock, I think. But then, suddenly, I understand what's happening, why this time is different—one straw too many; you're adding up betrayals like some arguing attorney.

"And Tragg, another of our *brothers?*—he made enough profit dealing dope to his friends to buy a hundred acres in the Berkshires last week."

A bitter glance in my direction and then you look away again. Moments pass, empty, silent; I have no rebuttal even if you wanted one. You reach up slowly and remove your arm band, dropping it beside the broken album.

"I've been thinking," you say softly then, the sarcasm drained from your voice; you close your eyes. I freeze, afraid; hear that drawbridge creaking shut on me. "I've been thinking that I want to get away."

I hesitate, too much at stake. "From me?" I hear myself say.

You look up, consider the question; a moment passes, nothing certain; then, the verdict: you shake your head. "From here," you say, taking my hand. "From all this shit."

My father, gaunt and slumped, an open-ended parenthesis, only nods, eyebrows rising another notch, when he's informed that we're planning to join a communal farm. My mother worries about dirt and trichinosis; your mother threatens to disown you, her letters wrapped in catechism pamphlets. But it's the summer of '70 and disappointments don't last; armed with new plans, revived ideals, we rebound with enthusiasm. Turning inward, to ourselves, our friends, the ones we trust, we're counting on building an alternative life, miles from the city where things went wrong.

Yes, it's summer all right, August twenty-third, to the best of my recollection around 7 P.M., the sun a wash of spilt crimson, settling in the gaps between the mountains, a single

15

star already risen and set like a gem in the cobalt blue of the eastern horizon. We stand, hand in hand, on the crest of a hill, ourselves set in the day's-end silence and solitude, below us a rock-pocked pasture with its encroaching thickets and dark green grasses and dead stump statues like crouching shepherds. Just arrived, on the brink of a new day, a new decade, this new life we plan to forge together. Just arrived and the air seems to breathe renewal, anything possible, the cool damp grasses and evening breezes of a land far removed from corrupt religion and political betrayal—we've escaped; free, we think; a second chance for the two of us. Just the first night of this farm life we've chosen for ourselves, and awed, we wait, daring to hope, hand in hand on the crest of a hill, learning the subtle shades that night can take in the pastured valleys of the Green Mountains.

Do you remember the scene, that August night in 1970? Do you see it as I do now, as the last happy frame in our tragic film—Jack and Jackie, smiling king and queen, in the back seat of their limousine, waving to the cheering Dallas crowds, unaware that a sniper's taking aim? We stand, hand in hand, the grasslands below, the sky color-streaked, not able to see the assassin's shadow in the distant trees or the still foreboding in the sunset's peace; not able to discern the sad secret within all things, no ironic half-smile to mask our features. Because it's the summer of '70 and we've not yet planted our crops too late or wrenched our backs on the rock-strewn land, not yet had serious discussions with our communal family about the "incestuous" infidelity that's running rampant. Because his Holiness has not yet arrived in America and my father's not taken his physical exam and Eddie Carlson still exists in the hope of his parents and on honor lists. Because you have not left me. Instead, together, on the crest of a hill, on the brink of our future, we wait, a liberated couple coming of age, armed with the right ideals for the wrong decade.

Exhibit 6d-13: two typewritten pages, stapled together, their contents single-spaced in pica-size letters. A document, apparently contractual in nature, its numbered articles subsumed under capitalized headings (Finances, Fidelity, Household Responsibilities), its language legalistic (". . . the party of the first part and the party of the second part do hereby and herewith enter into agreement . . ."), its contents finalized by two dated signatures. They're our signatures, yours and mine, Exhibit 6d-13 the "marriage" contract which you've drawn up in place of taking vows.

Because it's the spring of '73, and not yet aware that this is just a "phase," the necessary unleashing of your repressed anger, you no longer trust me; instead analyze my every word and action for the latent sexism you're certain infects me. No longer the parish paragon or even the Catholic liberal, you spit on the altars where you used to worship, on Teddy Kennedy and the Virgin Mary, while agonizing over your inability to feel comfortable with lesbianism. The communal farm deserted, we've moved to the city, to food co-ops and consciousness raising, to a contract detailing who on what day will water our azaleas. You take a seminar on Volkswagen repair; I learn how to patch holes in my pants. You begin law school at night; I join a men's group and learn how to cry—for I've not yet been shown that the feminist revolution is a Western illusion, that man and woman like yin and yang, though spiritually equal, must take opposite forms.

Meanwhile, back in Pennsylvania, Eddie Carlson's father has started a letter campaign, trying to reify the M.I.A.s; and for the first time in fifteen years, my father has stopped riding the 8:10 train—he's not allowed to, sent home by a company doctor for a battery of tests at the local hospital. As I'm told this over the phone, I sense the incipient hysteria behind my mother's optimism, the shadows of panic in her frequent

17

pauses; but when I ask her if I should come home, her nervous laughter cuts me off: "No need to, no need to." There is, though, and the morning of the day that the tests are to be completed, I know it—because I haven't slept at all that night, because I don't want to be told over long-distance telephone, because you have to take care of the people you care about.

And so I leave for Pennsylvania, arriving there in the late afternoon, wet from my six-hour hitch in the April rain, shoulders sore from my backpack's weight. No one seems home; no one answers my calls as I enter the back door, through the kitchen and into the dining room, pausing on the threshold of my father's study. There, I see him; ten feet away, my father sits in his favorite chair, bathrobe-wrapped, staring out a window and across the street to a seven-room house that mirror-images our own. Beside him, atop a card table, lie the scattered pieces of a jigsaw puzzle—uncompleted, unsolved. I wait while my father stares out, knowing not to speak, knowing that the time will come for him to acknowledge my presence there; I wait until the silence of the room is so complete that I can hear my mother's muffled crying from an upstairs bedroom. Then, finally, he turns toward the door, and with his secret eyes crowned by slightly arched brows, his lips flickering his painful half-smile, he says to me: "I should have believed the Surgeon General."

Two days later, you return to our apartment from a law school class and find me sitting on the living room sofa—alone, lights out, backpack still unpacked, staring out. Neither of us speaks for a moment; standing in the doorway, you let your book bag slide to the floor.

"How did it go?"

"He's dying," I say, surprised by it, the idea, the phrase; it's the first time I've said it aloud, and I'm tentative, startled by the words themselves, repeat them again as if practicing some exotic foreign idiom. "He's dying."

There's a pause and the pause is too long; by the time you start across the room, I've already imagined your internal response, a silent condemning analysis—macho-trapped, unable to express my emotions well, something like that—reduced to just another example to be discussed on Wednesday night by your women's group. You're beside me in a moment's time, but the comforting hand I'd been waiting for arrives too late. I push it away.

"I'd like to be alone, I think."

Yes, it's the spring of '73, spring of John Dean and Gordon Liddy, and my father still smiles and you still sleep in my bed and Eddie Carlson still lives in the hopes of his parents. But they're already there to be seen if we only knew how to read—the sentences of death, the endings predestined, assassins conspiring in their snipers' nests. The writing's already on the wall on that April day that I hitch home: on two typewritten pages stapled together, the strangled syntax of a love that's dying; on every pack of Viceroy cigarettes, the Surgeon General's printed warning.

Theory 9a: "The Void." There is no one following me; no plots exist. Nothing matters; nothing makes sense. Answers are illusions, questions foolish; you can't assassinate what's never been.

The Buddha is ten pounds of flax.

It's the fall of '76, fall of Jerry Ford and Jimmy Carter, red-white-and-blue place mats in every restaurant, Patty Hearst out on bail in her parents' apartment, town parades

19

instead of protest marches; and you have long since left me. The campuses sleep, Quaaludes replacing LSD, professional school applications quadrupling. Normalcy reigns everywhere: makeup and gossip columns, college proms and Bloomingdales. Soap operas run on prime-time television; King Kong climbs the World Trade Center; Eldridge Cleaver gives patriotic speeches and is praised in a column by William F. Buckley. Meanwhile, touring the country, paunched and balding like Frank Sinatra, the Beach Boys make their third or fourth comeback; and his Holiness proclaims a fast and retreat, a solemn celebration of the Year of the Lemur. Not yet aware of his secret connections to the C.I.A., I follow his Holiness's sacred orders, shaving my head, meditating each day an hour longer.

1976, October twenty-fifth, called home from the ashram at 9 P.M.; a midnight plane to Philadelphia, an early morning bus to suburbia, rushing up the street past dawdling school children—but it's already too late. He lies where he's died, on the couch of his study, beside a never completed jigsaw puzzle, too weak in the end to push its pieces, my mother forced to move them for him. Just a shell now, a parched pod, its seeds scattered, the mysteries gone—not passed on. And even though I know as Krishna told Arjuna in the *Bhagavad Gita* that suffering and death are unenlightened illusions, even though I'm silently chanting a mantra specially selected for the Year of the Lemur, I begin to sense on that October twenty-fifth a sudden dissolution of centeredness.

It's the fall all right, late October, just three months away from my thirtieth birthday, the ground still thawed for easier burial. The air's cool and damp, the cemetery grass soaking our feet, but the rain has stopped; and my mother, black-veiled, holds my arm as we're preached the promise of eternal

20

life. Before us the coffin, flower-adorned; behind us a platoon of huddled mourners, aunts and uncles, neighbors, business associates. Mrs. Carlson, whose son remains in perpetual suspension, whose husband still writes furious letters to congressmen and editors, stands nearby, wearing grief on her features like a housecoat and slippers.

Only at the end, after the final amen, do I notice your presence there; come late, in the last row of mourners, a fair and handsome business woman beside a fluted, water-stained mausoleum. Kind, a kind thing for you to do; taking the day off, riding the train in from New York, rushing by taxi to the cemetery. And so unexpected, over a year since I've had a letter from you, nearly two years since we've been together. We approach each other tentatively, like enemy soldiers in neutral territory, embarrassed by the changes we've made: you, in your conservative suit, a lawyer now, token conscience for some conglomerate; me with my head shaved, my fingers colored by incense stains, not yet aware that I'm a brainwashed dupe of his Holiness. A couple liberated, a couple separated, come of age, feeding on the strange and bitter fruit of this unexpected decade, making small talk together in a Pennsylvania cemetery. "The sixties are over," you finally say, trying to explain away my saffron robe and your memo-stuffed briefcase. "Priorities have changed."

I nod my head (who can argue with that?), glancing away, nothing to say. But you're not finished yet, come here to confess, to admit that 1973, with its marriage contract and caviling, was not a proud year; a "phase," you say, the unfortunate but necessary unleashing of your anger. And I apologize too, for my defensiveness, for not fully understanding the changes you were going through. We're so polite, exchanging our confessions there on the wet grass of the cemetery, on the cool gray day that my father is buried; so polite and shy until my mother calls my name from the waiting limousine. I turn, about to leave, but you reach out, hand to my hand, holding on, squeezing tight—a kind thing for you to do.

"I'm sorry," you say, your eyes embracing more than the grave. "For everything."

"I know—me too."

And we stand there for a moment, holding hands, comfort from a friend for a grieving son—no more than that, the urge long gone. Not even the hurt remains; it's hard to believe, but everything, even the pain has left. Who could have foreseen that on a fall day in '76 your touch would mean nothing more than sympathy, that such strong feelings could be so dead?

"But where . . . ?" I begin to say; my mother calls again and I turn away. Duty-drawn, I take a backward step, shaking my head, no words for the question I need to ask.

But you know what I mean, and the slight smile you give me then holds all the answers if only I could decipher it—the same smile my father learned on the 8:10 special to Philadelphia, the same smile Eddie Carlson learned while being trained to kill by the United States Army. Bitter and resigned, mocking and self-mocking all at the same time. Innocence betrayed; irony, the survivor's stock-in-trade.

"Dallas," you say, "Dealey Plaza, just beyond the School Book Depository."

It's the fall of '63, Friday, November twenty-second; in Dallas, at Dealey Plaza, on Elm Street just beyond the Texas School Book Depository; a day of history, of recorded images, pictures imprinted on the nation's consciousness by the fortuitous camera of Abraham Zapruder. It's Friday, November twenty-second, 12:30 P.M., a specific frame of the Zapruder film, the act already committed, three shots fired, brain tissue splattered on the windshield, on the seats, on the raspberry-colored suit of Jackie Kennedy. The act's been committed, the New Frontier receding, Camelot invaded, violated, our innocence dying on the back seat of a presidential limousine.

It's all there to be seen in just one frame of color film, the shock and horror of infamy, the urge to resist reality: the gleaming black curves of the president's car, a hero's chariot, flag-adorned; the green grass and flinching spectators; the man himself, slumped and bleeding; and, too, dominating the scene in her raspberry suit and pillbox hat, Mrs. Jacqueline Bouvier Kennedy. Fighting back, risking all, either an assassin's bullet or a calamitous fall, she climbs onto the rear of the speeding car, and reaching out now, tries to retrieve from the rear bumper of the limousine a shorn piece of her husband's skull. Yes, it's all there to be seen, such a human response to the tragedy, a perfect image of the country's yearning—Mrs. Jacqueline Bouvier Kennedy reaching back, trying to retrieve the jagged pieces of our shattered dream as if she, we, could make it whole again.

It's then that I appear, a new figure entering the scene, one discovered only recently by the latest photographic enhancement techniques. It's then that I glide into view, sprinting full speed from the borders of the film, man of the moment, a mythic figure of angular body and lightning reactions, of refined sensibilities and relentless purpose. Come to save a life, a president, a generation's idealism; an historical revisionist about to redo a decade of our existence. Our every daydream's reified hero, sprinting up Elm Street in a three-piece suit.

I leap, a striking vision of vigor and grace, onto the rear of the speeding limousine on that Friday afternoon in the fall of

'63, and there, risking all, either an assassin's bullet or a calamitous fall, I help our First Lady with her singular mission, gathering piece after piece of our shattered leader. From the windshield, from the seats, from the stained skirt of the raspberry suit, his shards are scraped, then placed on the smooth black rear of the limousine, where they are carefully sorted by color and shape—the two of us pausing above them then as above the strewn pieces of the jigsaw puzzle which my father worked on in his deathroom study. And together, through patience and cunning, through the exhausting process of trial and error, we, myself and Jackie Kennedy, precariously balanced on that limousine, do what all the king's horses and all the king's men and all the conspiracy theorists have never done: we put Saint Jack back together again. We fit the pieces, solve the puzzle. We assassinate history and rescue the sixties.

And all the crowds cheer, the parade route lined with ecstatic Texans, whistles and waving, blizzards of confetti, a roar of appreciation rising across the nation. Teachers in their classrooms pledging allegiance; farmers in their fields, businessmen in their boardrooms, sighing relief; parish paragons, their knees locked beneath the skirts of their Catholic school uniforms, drying the tears in their eyes. Because it's the fall of '63 and we've just put Saint Jack back together again, saving the day, turning us away from a mean and vulgar sidetrack of history.

And there will be peace again throughout the land, no need for protest, no anger or hatred, bigotry overcome by our rescued leader: Dr. King, Jack, Ted, and Bobby Kennedy, Governor Wallace and Mary Jo Kopechne, playing game after game of touch football together on the compound lawn in Hyannisport. And there will be no riots or assassinations, no

24

Viet Nam War to snatch away our neighbors, Eddie Carlson driving up and down our streets, patching rubber irresponsibly, without ever having to learn an ironic half-smile, without ever being reduced to a vague shadow of his parents' hope. And my father will not have to ride his 8:10 train, will not have to hide those secrets in his eyes while withering away in self-imposed silence; we'll spend days, whole days together, father and son, bonded by love, on the worn wooden steps of our shaded back porch, talking to each other, uncovering the secrets, fatherly advice for the heir apparent. Because it's the fall of '63 and Saint Jack's been put back together again; and the leaders I revere will not betray me; and the values I believe in will not change; and the people I love will live forever; and through sickness and health and all the necessary phases, through all the crimson-streaked sunsets of Camelot's days, hand in my hand, you will not leave me.

Psalm

N THE CAR, HIS IMMENSE AND HAIRLESS hands melding with the steering wheel, David accelerated into the bank of the curve, weight shifting, the outside wheels lifting, giddying him for a moment with gravity's loss, caught as if in a morning dream of flight, his fear giving way to intimations of immortality; not an idea but a feeling, an hormonal surge: mistakes couldn't be made . . . this was real. Invincible then, the car held the curve, flexing rubber and steel, gathering momentum for the straightaway; then righting itself, it flung down the highway like a sure stroke across canvas or like a spring thaw's river rush, sluicing through the scoured channels, cutting across the stone shadows of the valley, beneath the tilting, rock-strewn pastures and their never-startled cows, Hindu with tranquillity. David drew in a breath, his perfect moment burst by pulses of self-consciousness: it *had* been real, and "beauty" was a word for the feeling, or "fate" for philosophizing men; "grace" had an even nicer ring, every prop in its appointed place, an artist's eye directing things. But Carol, no child of light, couldn't understand the seductive promise of sunrise on a mountain road.

"Would you *please* slow down?"

Her glance was accusing, but drained of surprise; an old argument, not a new one—the shorthand fights of long-lived marriages. And she couldn't really turn to him anyway, Del curled on her lap, safe and womb-wrapped, as if he had never been born. (A painting: *Madonna and Child*; all womankind with wanly luminous skintones and worried eyes, protecting the boy-child. In chiaroscuro, faint heaven beams irradiating the family; a stranger in the darker foreground, though, whose very shadow was the promise of a cross, of split palms and a crown of thorns. One couldn't paint it now, of course; sentimental, they'd say. But a mother, even Carol, was an artist anyway, and traditional, sculpting herself despite what was fashionable into all the age-old poses: "protecting the boy-child." Someday, David thought, someday the drama will be perfected and we won't be forced to act it out.)

"We're late," he said.

"Better late . . ." Carol snapped, then paused, panicking (*"step on the crack and you'll break your back"*), avoiding the words; and they hung in the air like a bad joke between them. To see her like this, unsure and hesitant—Carol, career rationalist, suddenly superstitious—was to lose one's compass, the North Star slipping, Newton purged by Relativity; nothing certain anymore. She won't make it through this, David suddenly thought, stunned by the thought: that *he* should prove the stronger one. His right hand, paint-daubed, reached out, crossing the seat, touching her arm, feeling the slight tremor of her silent sobbing; quiet comfort, a measure of sharing as the car slipped past a stretch of forest. Removing his hand to make a turn, he listened dully to the rustling of Kleenex within her purse. The surge was gone now, not a trace of immortality left, and he felt awkward and small, an insect dodging the wrath of God, his hands wrapped tightly around the steering wheel as if afraid he'd lose control. Early morning light flickered through the valley, the sun flirting with the mountainous skyline, the car one moment bright and warm, then cast between stone walls, cliff-sides veined with quartz and moss, David drowning in their dark wet shadows as though sunk to the bottom of a well. He would accelerate then, surfacing for air, urging the car forward toward the next patch of light, and there, warming his skin like some priestly palm of ritual forgiveness, the sun would calm him. It would end quickly, his relief always transient, the highway's insinuating ribbon—an abstraction of the river running beside it—soon shrouded in shadows again. But time was on his side in this at least, the sun rising above the shading ridge.

They drove on in silence, past landmarks grown familiar on their twice-weekly trips to the city: Top Hat Rock, strips of pine-redolent forest, and eventually, Mantle Falls, which had been frozen solid just six weeks ago, tucked away then in a nave of the cliff-face like some church figurine; pure white, chaste spirituality—a Brancusi rendering of the Virgin Mary. But it was melted now, rent and violated, water bruising the rocks with its suicidal plunge, spraying even the road. Last week, David had told Del that a little bearded man lived behind the falls (Carol frowning all along: just another Santa Claus myth to be debunked later on). God's gremlin, he'd called him; an habitual mischief-maker and tormentor of adults, who fed on the feathery gills beneath mushroom caps, who thrived on surprise and practical jokes, stealing pies from window sills, thwarting all the well-laid plans of mice and men. Wide-eyed, Del, who'd met his first mouse the day before, an occasion then for solemn awe, had absorbed it all. And when David glanced at him now (curled, thumb to his lips, oblivious to the roar of the gremlin's den, to his last cruel trick, so safe it seemed), he floated, momentarily dislocated, his eye denying the mind's authority: no, this couldn't be happening.

"Which one is it going to be this time?" he said, eyes on the road again.

31

Carol sighed, stared straight ahead. "Don't you know by now?"

"I don't care about the names, the chemicals—it's what they do." He waited, but she wasn't going to answer him. "Is it the one that makes him sick?" he finally asked.

"I gave you the pamphlets; the least you could do is read them, remember the names."

"Why?"

"*Why?* Because he's your son, because . . ." Del stirred with the rise in Carol's voice, blinked open eyes too big for his body, overweening almost; like a cave animal's at night, luminous and watchful. David smiled at him. Carol pulled him closer, cast a reproachful, silencing glance in David's direction: *now look what you've done.* "You go back to sleep now, Honey."

Minutes passed, sun-bathed, as they crossed a stretch of open land; the river slowed, the valley wider, furrowed fields flanking the highway, an erumpent green from rich black soil. The heat of the day, fuel for the new hay, rippled the air, the valley coiled and swelling in the sunlit morning like a poised bud on the verge of unfolding. A thousand paintings here; the key was to capture the incipient violence behind the sun-steamed stillness. ("Floral," Gertz would sneer to his pallid coterie, "rebaked Turner; rural romanticism.") A sign, directing skiers to an "internationally famous" beef-and-beer restaurant, jutted from a field like a cartoon tag on a Ruisdael landscape.

"I did read them," David said at last, trying to acquit himself. The charge had been absurd but hurt anyway. Guilt worked like that, as unreasonable as love; he watched with amazement the things it made him do, an actor still, driven

32

through these scenes even as he sensed their futility. The competition between them now; more Carol's doing, but his fault too: who would put Del to bed, who would make his dinner or dress him in the morning—a reward in heaven for the more attentive parent. But at heart their game was a self-made penance, a desperate hope that duty made a difference.

"Let's not get into it," Carol said.

"It's just that the reasons don't matter; the physiology, the terms, they don't sink in. It's the effect; it's what's happening to . . ."

"*David,*" Carol warned, glancing toward Del; seemed with a subtle shift of her arms and lap to brandish him like a threat: *protecting the boy-child.*

"He knows, damn it," David said, not angry but impatient, sorry though that he had spoken. The illusion, after all, was for their own sake, for the parents—the pretense that they were shielding him. Del knew, all right, and better than they did; not the idea but the reality. It was happening to him, for him it was real, without the terms, the Latin-stiff phraseology; like the sun on his arm: felt. But watching himself and amazed by it, David played Carol's game, uttered his lie automatically when he saw Del stirring, coming awake.

"You *do* know the farm song, don't you, Del?"

Del rubbed his eyes, sitting up in his mother's lap. "Sheep," he said.

"That's right," David nodded, then cleared his throat, waving his arm, a massive blond-flecked baton, directing his family in a diverting song as if this were vacation time. Carol's soprano, clean and note-perfect; David's baritone a barroom bellow; Del, as always, hopelessly out of tune, improvising the words as he went along, half-asleep still:

33

The sheep lay low
in the fields at night;
the shepherds watch over them
while they sleep tight.

The cows lay low
in the fields at night . . .

A lullaby, child-simple, its verses virtually endless in number; a Noah's ark of possibilities sung to David by his paternal grandmother. And now passed on, quatrained comfort, from father to son, a tradition of sorts . . . ending. Glancing toward Carol, noting her false cheer, her pretended smile, the only kind she gave him now—and for Del's sake—David sang louder, a mere mortal, awkward and small, for a moment a child himself again, focusing on the words of his grandmother's song: *The horses lay low / in the fields at night . . .*

(A painting: *The Lullaby*; a grandmother rocking a cradle-hidden child, her face averted, everything shown by the line of her shoulders—the weight of sadness, age's erosion. Beyond them, dwarfing the cupped shell of their intimacy, an infinite backdrop, a tundra-bare moonscape of desolation, of unfocused danger; all the implied threat of di Chirico. ["Allegorical," Gertz would groan while painting beige squares on an off-white background.]) If he . . . if he could only paint it, he might understand, might believe that this was happening: Del lying down on his mother's lap, falling back asleep with the sheep and the cows, the two shepherds watching over him songless now, everything shown by their averted eyes, their dying smiles, by the shepherd's-crook slump of Carol's neck.

Speeding through the last tapering stem of the valley, up a

serpentine stretch of highway, the car reached the top of the last mountain pass, pausing there as if to catch its breath, the air through its vents palpably cooler. From that vantage point, one could see miles to the south and west; trace the slow death of the mountain range through a series of ever diminishing hills to a flattened, fertile river plain. A reticle of roads—gray filaments, conduits of motion—cut the land there into the patterned plots of suburbia, where trees, sparse and pruned, were individual monuments instead of riotous colonies. Breathless, as though he had climbed and not driven to this spot above the last tree tops, David thrilled to the expanse of scenery. In the past, living in the city, he had tended to forget about waterfalls and sunsets, their sensual reality; and now, living in the mountains, he tended to forget about the paved face of civilization. But here, midway, brought to the top of the range's last peak, overlooking suburbia, the city's spire-pricked haze hanging in the distance, here one could see them all, the contrasting styles, the landscapes of living. It over-whelmed David, moved him, this visual panoply, its scope and complexity, its wash of colors and multiple forms, a world more varied and subtle than the mind could absorb. Theories evaporated given a view like this. And forced twice a week now to make this trip, he felt like some ultimate commuter, a latter-day Odysseus: starting in the country, in their mountain cabin, its knotty pine walls lined with partridge feathers; speeding through the suburbs, reason's dreamland, where every block was a perfect garden; on to the city, that hot hub of violence and creativity, Prometheus unbound, man indifferent to the will of the gods, forging a life in his own tragic image. The canvas complete, everything seen in a three-hour ride from mountains to city.

As he gazed to the south over the steering wheel, David felt that surge again, safe and invincible, his awe filling the open spaces in an extension of himself. There was secret order here, a hint of Providence, the sky itself describing, defining the scene below with a natural metaphor in light and motion: from the east, the sun, immense and rising; from the west, a squat gray line of advancing clouds, consuming the sky's cerulean field like locust swarms. Imminent collision—light and dark, fire and water—all the range of possibilities laid out before him. That this sky could exist, and above this scene, fitting it so well, that David could see it and make the connection, seemed a reason for hope, an assurance of meaning, the world a better place—all the promises of beauty. But made aware again of Del and Carol, David suddenly checked his enthusiasm: life was not just a distant, silent panorama, but here and now, and in motion, his family caught up in the irresistible propulsion of their own small drama.

Pushed past the peak, the car began its winding descent, gravity-drawn a bit too fast, momentum checked by stabs at the brake; and laden with guilt, David sank too, trying to conceal the slight smile that had shaped his lips. Perhaps Carol hadn't noticed, but he was afraid to look, knowing all too well the expression on her face, its accusing rage: how dare, *how dare* you enjoy yourself! That night, months ago now, when they had taken a walk across the snow, the sky ice-clear, infinite with stars, that was the night she had begun her rule of gloom, the night she had started resenting him. He had smiled then, too, had dared a child's response to the clarity of the stars—simple awe—but Carol couldn't forgive him for it, or forgive the sky. They were crucifying her boy, you see, and as in some cinematic version of the Easter story, she demanded earthquake tremors, rage from heaven, thunder and lightning over Calvary. The whole world should mourn her loss, rent hair, wear sackcloth; but instead, either dumb or unattending, life continued on, not a single beat missed, like the industrious ship in Breughel's *Icarus:* indifferent to the fall. It wasn't David's fault that the stars shone on; he was a witness, not a cause. He loved Del too, as much as Carol, would do anything to make him well again *(absurd, absurd the things guilt made him say and do, the over-explaining, the self-justifications)*; it was just that he knew what couldn't be done, an expert in mankind's impotence.

"What time is it?" David said, desperate for small talk, one shepherd to another; although they constantly fought now, they still shared the same flock, the same space, fate—lonely together.

"Ten to eight."

"We'll make it on time then if the traffic's not bad."

"Depends on the bridge."

"I suppose so. They should have finished paving it by now, though."

Carol nodded, David gestured with his free hand, the car flew out of the mountain's last curve, spiraling down to the level of the sea. A domestic scene, they were playing at normality, pretending they were in control of things; but meanwhile, perched on their shoulders, with the singsong taunting of a playground bully, the gremlin undid their tapestried lies, his whispers haunting their uneasy silences: *"Nothing is certain, nothing is certain!"* Systems were illusions, cockalorum bluffs against the darkness; chaos ruled everywhere, gyrating chance and random disaster; justice was the joke of vulpine tyrants, a rationale for their power. David shook his head, picked at azure flecks of paint on his hand, squeezed the wheel harder when Carol mentioned the treatment again. (*"Nothing is certain, nothing is certain!"*) They said, David remembered, that Del's hair might fall out.

"Dr. Stein brought up that Seattle experiment again,"

Carol said, cautious, testing him; wanting, David thought, for him to respond with optimism. Trying to please, he nodded his head.

"It's just a matter of time, he said. They're on the right track, Dr. Stein thinks." Carol caught her breath; her voice, tinsel-bright at first, was asthmatic and quick. "But just how long it will take, no one can say." Another pause, a plummet into panicking. "You can't put science on a preset timetable."

Awful, her parroting of these waiting room nostrums, hollow phrases for the layman's comfort; it made David feel sad and small, and he turned to Carol now, afraid that she might break down again. His glance, though, was sun-blinded, Carol's hair an Impressionist burst of reflected light; color routing form, boundaries exploded with golds and reds that were textured, warm—the eye's first blur on a fine fall morning. But then came the focusing—surface wasn't everything—dazzle giving way to the etched lines of suffering. She wasn't taking it well, this gremlin's prank; cosmic jokes were beyond her, black humor not in her repertoire, helplessness a state she refused to believe in, preferring the idol of Modern Medicine. She was better with people, with the politics of living; Carol would have never, for example, let Gertz force her from the university as David had. But when it came to the universe—her father's funeral, Del's diagnosis—problems not solvable by ad hoc committees or tireless lobbying, she was as lost as David at a faculty meeting. Yes, David thought, sure of it now, he *was* the stronger one here; within their marriage, following the efficient logic of specialization, catastrophes were his responsibility. But how to comfort her and Del, how to get through these months himself? There would be no pamphlet explaining that, he knew; no imminent Seattle miracle.

"They've made more progress," Carol said, looking away from him, "they've made more progress in the last two years than in the entire decade preceding them."

It was an article of faith, her new catechism; David heard it at least once a day, knew the lines by heart, stanza after stanza (*the sheep lay low in the fields at night*) of Carol's personal lullaby.

"Yes, I remember Dr. Stein saying that."

"And they say that the Anselm treatment has possibilities."

"Yes," David said (what else could he do?), "I saw that in the article you gave me."

Carol glanced at him quickly, seeming to doubt her own illusions, seeming to sense their sure futility. She struggled, though, to maintain her front, her self-protecting desperate bluff, asking herself, "Does he really believe that?", wanting him to because if he did, then she might too. Her accusation was a self-accusation now, unreasonable guilt better than an unreasonable world. She had been a working mother, con-scientious teacher; the style of the times, of course, but in their family the arrangement seemed natural, David home painting and the more patient of the two anyway. But then the judgment had been rendered, a grave condemnation from the prophet doctors who bore clipboard reports like Mt. Sinai tablets, and she had turned on herself, a suddenly backsliding feminist. *Her fault, her fault*—a woman of reason, who had to have causes, began with herself; hating her job now as if it were the proved carcinogen, bearing her career like a scarlet letter. And when she stared at him like this, David knew that she half wanted him to express her silent guilt, to voice the bitter accusation inside herself (*Bad mother, bad mother!*); knew, too, though, that to do so would be kinder than to tell her what he really suspected, than to whisper sadly what the

39

gremlin chanted: *You had, you have, no control, no control; nothing you could have done would have mattered at all.* But David refused to believe it himself, his eye denying what his mind knew to be true. And so he said nothing, ignored these invitations, forfeited his responsibility—painted pictures of silence, frame after frame, in their speeding car.

"Dr. Stein says that the Russians are trying a different approach."

"Yes," David said, nodding his head, the car growing dim, the sun smothered by the first froward cloud, "yes, I remember him saying that."

(A painting: *The Rush Hour;* gray cement and granite squares, right angular order everywhere; simple slash strokes for the crowds of people, angled forward in frenetic motion. And yet, a watercolor, its forms dissolving, seen as if through a rain-streaked window; all Platonic shadows, an opiate dreamland, with the city melting into puddles of color, its pastels fading to a wan chimera . . . *this is not happening!*) Del stirred again on his mother's lap; David's eyes flicked between the road and his son; the pavement stretched on, taut and resolute; a solitary cow, Chagall-surreal, pathetic remnant of the valley farms, chewed grass beside a split-level house. (Were there causes to all of this?) Lot after lot, stroke by stroke, the suburban streets adjacent to the road described themselves: eighteenth-century optimism mass-produced.

"Mommy," Del said, "could I have some apple?"

His parents, co-conspirators, exchanged warning glances, silent reminders to play their game, to deny without telling why, hoping Del wouldn't figure it out.

"Mommy . . ."

"You wait a little bit, Honey."

"*Now,* Mommy, I want some apple *now.*"

"Did you see your mouse this morning, Del?" David interrupted.

Del shook his head. Already a manipulator, he knew he should keep his eyes on Carol, but the bait too tempting, he vacillated, his head rotating between his parents.

"I think he was looking for you," David added.

The hook was set; Del turned on his mother's lap. "In the barn?"

"That's right."

Del considered this, glancing over Carol's shoulder as if their barn might still be glimpsed through the wide back window. "Is that his home?"

"I think so. He seems to spend a lot of time in there."

Del frowned, a parent himself now, worrying. "But won't he get cold at night?"

"He's got fur to keep him warm. And all that straw to burrow in. You remember his fur, don't you, Del?"

Del nodded his head. David sighed, relaxing inside; the diversion was working. If they could keep Del preoccupied, he might forget that he couldn't eat, might not deduce the reason why—until the bridge at least. There, David's strategies never worked; there, Del's cries would begin in earnest, aware of what would happen to him.

"I tell you, Del, you and that mouse are getting so close, it's about time we came up with a name for him."

Del liked the idea; Carol too—grateful that the crisis had been averted, but jealous as well, David knew. It should have been *her* game that Del wanted to play, Carol still competing, still trying to earn her expiation with proven acts of motherhood . . . but there wasn't much time to amass good deeds, and when the time came, she had no God, beyond her own conscience, to present them to. David grew silent, let Carol

41

take over, the game's emcee, a concession to her anxiety. Instead, he drove on, entranced, withdrawn, the highway's stripes his only guide, their broken lines pulsing before him like some endlessly repeated Morse code mantra (*"nothing is certain, nothing is certain, all is illusion"*). Above him, on either side of the highway, hidden by fences and flowering shrubbery, middle-class houses peeked out at the morning, the lanes now thick with their commuting owners who were drawn like filings to the magnet city. No control, no control; caught in a stream and surrendering to its flow; no control at all, it seemed. ("Whiskers," Carol suggested, but Del resisted, searching for something more appropriate.) Hearing them like this, Madonna and Child in a scene so normal, so domestic, that he could hardly believe that . . . *remission* was the term that they used; not remission of sins but of symptoms, the signs that made the diagnoses seem true. Fool's gold, false hope, being held in abeyance like this, poised for the fall; always, ever in the waiting room. And Carol clinging to these scientific journals; on her knees, praying to Seattle. What would happen to her when the cures fell through, when the symptoms reappeared as they were predicted to? His job, it was *his* job to get them through this, to handle the universe, to come out of the studio and guide his family, *his* responsibility to be the realist. But that wasn't a style that he painted in.

"David," Carol said.

"I'm sorry, what were you saying?"

"Del wants to know what you think of 'Wiggles' as a name."

David glanced down, a mock stern father, paterfamilias, considering a plea from one of his subjects; Del's eyes were wide, his brows raised, locked into silent, solemn expectation. Such a serious little boy—but then, who could blame him?

"You mean like this?" David said, reaching out, tickling

Del in his vulnerable spot, beneath the arm. Del wriggled wildly, let out an hilarious scream—"Daaadeee!"—even Carol laughing with him; but their perfect moment was ended quickly with a warning cry from the family's sentry.

"Oh, God," Carol said, staring through the windshield, pointing ahead, "they haven't finished paving it yet."

David looked up; they were still two miles away from "it," the bridge, a word not mentioned when Del was awake; he knew what it meant: just fifteen minutes to the hospital. The traffic had already slowed, the three lanes filled, and from their vantage point atop the last suburban hill, they could see the lines of motionless cars leading up to the river, the city's border. Carol glanced at her watch nervously.

"How much time have we got?"

"Forty minutes," she said.

David sped up, maneuvered the car, switching lanes, darting quickly for the open spaces, his role now reduced to this specific task—getting Del to the clinic on time. But for all his efforts, his sudden turns and yanking accelerations, they barely gained on the surrounding cars; the traffic slowly clotted around them until, at last, they were forced to a stop.

"Damn it," Carol said as the lane to their left started moving again. David drummed the steering wheel, shifted in his seat impatiently—stuck at the gate, heart beating fast, unable to race, and there was nothing he could do about it. No control, trapped in this stream, a prisoner to its flow, Del confused and staring at him, worried by their sudden shift in mood. They said, David remembered while glancing at him, that Del would lose his hair, become a little old man, bald and sere, the course of a lifetime in one short year; nature tricked, disease an attack on its symmetry.

"Why don't you lie down?" David said to Del, affecting a

43

smile, afraid that he would soon catch sight of the bridge. Carol reached out, took Del in her arms, but he twisted, resisting, refused to put his head on her lap. Perhaps he already knew, but David couldn't be sure as the traffic began moving in fits and starts, the lanes merging from three to two, cars directed by flashing arrows. They were descending now, past the peak of the hill, the city stretching below them on the flattened lowlands like a table set with brick and concrete, a bittersweet, smoke-steaming feast of achievement and excess. Carol struggled to keep Del on her lap; the breeze through the vents was tinged with exhaust; the clouds, racing ahead, had broken ranks, the ground mottled with their silhouettes. In his mind's eye, David suddenly saw Gertz—his larva lips, wet-white and curling, the raised brow of his triumphant cynicism—and he reached out then, unaccountably afraid, caressing Del with a clumsy stroke, a dog's-paw groping of his thigh; conscience-struck: *Bad father, bad father!* He should be able to do something more, should, with a flick of his brush, a knowing stroke, be able to change the canvas before them. Dumb instinct, Gertz would call the urge; others would say love. But the words didn't matter; whichever was used, he still had to, wanted to, play the part, act it out. A parent, father. "Protecting the boy-child."

"Mommy?"

"Sssh," Carol said. "You try to sleep now."

The traffic edged forward with a kind of surly insistence, bumper to bumper, no space spared, territorial warfare, the lanes reduced again from two to one. Sealed behind glass and steel, commuters smoked cigarettes and checked their watches, shifted nervously in their suit jacket uniforms as they were funneled slowly toward the umbilical bridge. Rats, Gertz would say, performing in their maze; ritual frustration—but there were paintings here, stories. David kept his eyes on Del as the car drew closer, on a plane now with the city and dwarfed by it: if Del raised his head above the dash, he would see the bridge and the play would be finished, their pretense of happiness smashed. ("We lie like this because we love you, Son." But there would be no "someday" when Del would understand them.)

They stopped again, two hundred yards before the bridge, the wind suddenly dead, the air humming with the squelched explosion of idling engines; rank combustion, diesel stench. Two of the bridge's three lanes were closed; and there, men leaned on shovels, trucks dumping gravel, a jackhammer busting pavement, thundering the morning; cops kibbitzed with hard-hat foremen. A boy, power-drunk, with a tyrant's strut, waved an orange flag, controlling the traffic like a water tap: on, then off; forward, then stopped / on, then off; forward, then stopped. Here, in the city again, amid all these people, all these engines, diminished by the abstract and angular skyline before them . . . David waited, an uneasy vigil, eyes rotating between the bridge and his son, who struggled now on Carol's lap, wanting to sit up, wanting to see, to know; a child's curiosity, the killer of innocence. Outside, flanking the bridge, the river's wide green channel was tinged with gray, and funereally still, a few boats, their sails deflated, waiting for gusts to fill them again. A pause, life for a moment not moving on; the stillness guarded by the sentinel clouds, squatting separate and full above the city.

Trapped there, distracted by his worrying, by a sinking suspicion that everything around him would collapse, disintegrate ("Don't look, don't look, Del! What you can't see, you won't know, so close your eyes, keep your head down—it's all illusion anyway" . . . *this is not happening!*), David's eye was drawn back to the sky, the lighting changed, the river cast in an odd and haunting atmosphere. An artist by habit, he noted the difference, how the air, suddenly dimmed and color-tinged, was caught in a visual paradox: the morning twilit. Low in the sky, an immense and billowing cloud had formed, veiling the sun, its bellied center faintly roseate and glowing, a halo quality about its edges. The surrounding sky was fissured with blue, its smaller clouds, partial mirrors, pink-cast too, and shimmering, as if suffused with imminent divinity—as in those religious paintings of the Early Renaissance where angels burst from resplendent clouds like winged seeds from a ripe pod, announcing miracles. David stared, struck by his own revelation: those skies, those skies in the paintings were real! One forgot, one tended to forget . . . God, to have a canvas now, to hold a brush, to capture this light, its aura of ominousness . . . Soaring now, David turned on his seat; the experience not shared or painted was incomplete; but there, a more sobering vision greeted him. Wrenched from the air and plummeting, the wax wings of his immortality, the smile on his lips shriveling: how dare, *how dare.* you . . .

Carol clutched a Kleenex in her fist, head slumped, lips pursed. Del had won their battle, bitten the apple; sitting up beside her now, he knew where he was, knew what would soon happen to him: a little old man, homunculus, facing premature indignities. Sad but brave, he tried not to cry, the brunt of a joke he was helpless to fight; just a passenger, after all, in the car, in life; in remission now, waiting for a sign, given his window, the world streaming by. David glanced from the boy to the sky, from the sky to the boy, the traffic on, then off; forward, then stopped / on, then off; forward, then stopped. Within one sweep of his eye, the limits were defined, joy and despair, a continuum implied: one picture after another, one more luminescent cloud or romantic setting, one more rat-bitten child or vomit-spewed canvas, Renoir and Brueghel, everything included. It was *real*, all of it—the mountains, the suburbs, the city, all the "schools," the styles of living, even Gertz with his tepid beige squares, his academic nihilism—*real*, all of it, *incredibly*, all part of the picture: Del was dying.

Stopped by the bridge, by the substance of things, David stared as the world waited on: the boats, their slackened sails; the clouds overhead; his wife's impatience (where was the miracle?); the worm of disease, the gremlin's planted seed, still uncurling. A thousand dramas incomplete. Behind him, car after car began to honk, the pompous flagman waving him on, the path now cleared, the bridge in all its inevitability waiting for them. But David refused to move on, gathering awe, his eyes still rotating between his son and the sky, his response to be drawn. A song-maker, picture-painter, witness to it all ("I saw this and it was real!")—an artist of amazement. But a shepherd, a father too. And now given this cloud, the cup of his senses overflowing.

With a sweep of his arm, he gathered Del up, the herd of cars bleating their horns, the furious flagman waving them on—impatient life, the world unaware that a boy was falling from the sky. Carol called his name. David nodded his head, had a message for them, his wife and son, as his finger pointed to the sky above.

"Look at the cloud," he said, lifting Del up, guiding his sight (in the car, beside the still waters, before the city of his enemies); an artist and father playing his part. "Look at the light."

Dice

1

AN AIRPORT, AMERICAN PERHAPS OR CANA-dian, exuding all the glossed sterility of public build-ings: fields of linoleum; plastic seats in gravestone rows; lines here and there shuffling forward; disembodied voices, like the robot agents of some higher order, directing the crowd with coded numbers; and, in some heretofore inconse-quential corner, inching along on a conveyer belt, an unobtru-sive suitcase stuffed with explosives. Mrs. M—— and her daughter Y—— rush by taxi to the smog-beshrouded flatlands where the airplanes lie. Mr. Q——, a teacher perhaps or a tax accountant, sleeps later than he wished, unaware that his bro-ken alarm clock will save his life. In a waiting room, a group of passengers, allegorically diverse—men and women, blacks and whites, newlyweds and octogenarians; the hodgepodge cast of some disaster film—sip rancid coffee from plastic cups or idly skim news magazines. Webs of circumstance, of coincidence link them up, their most innocuous decision (which line to take, which time) suddenly profound, saved or damned by the whim of a moment. Mrs. M—— and her daughter Y—— rushing toward the airport, trying to make their flight; an unob-trusive suitcase stuffed with explosives inching toward the plane they wish to fly; a mechanical voice, fate's middling-level bureaucrat, calling out a number to the unsuspecting crowd. And, heard everywhere, the perpetual busyness of leather on linoleum: a clatter of feet like rolling dice.

51

Or . . . a doorway, portal to a crowd, a singles bar or perhaps mansion party where beauty and money stalk each other, "producers" exchanging stares with teenage girls. T—— (or V—— or J—— or C——) stands in this doorway on the party's fringe, savoring the possibilities in front of him: women, so many of them, their inviting shapes, their intoxicating scents, their musical grace; women everywhere, to be watched, to be touched, to be kissed and sucked, to be admired, approached, seduced, discussed. For him, men don't exist, pockets of dead space, bland frames for this exotic display of femininity. There's a gold chain around his neck, some rough-hewn object hanging from it; a thick moustache above his lip, or perhaps a full beard, neatly trimmed. Add a leather coat or a denim jacket, a bright print shirt, its collar open, and the plumage is complete, the pose achieved, a titillating rogue masculinity; a neon warning, half-threat, half-promise: I-will-hurt-you-and-you-will-like-it. Waiting. In a doorway. This succulent anticipation of the hours before him. Women, the "now" of them, the night's potential running like a long-nailed finger down the seam of his stomach. And before his rapt and fascinated eyes, the party churns its feminine tide, a sea of sylphidine possibilities like so many numbers on a roulette wheel—which will be his?

Or . . . a boy, sprinting at first, an explosive burst after a boring morning behind a desk, rushing toward home and a waiting lunch, to a mother's planted kiss and inquiring eyes. He runs, this boy, eleven years old or maybe twelve, across a lot or across a field, running away or running toward, the weight of the future chasing him down. These strange feelings, his rioting body, these new possibilities, a million sperm dying on his hand: M——, who wears a brassiere, who makes him blush whenever she's near; the teachers in school who badger him already about preparing for college; his mother, her perplexing moods, those strange cries he hears behind her bedroom door . . . God, to be grown up or to have stayed a child, to be at the end once instead of always on the verge; God, to know what will happen before it occurs . . . He runs, this boy, he runs as if to hurry up time, out of school, across a backyard, avoiding the retiree crossing guard; down a main street, faster still, his path calibrated by utility poles. And as he hears a car approaching from the rear, he turns his fast dash home into an imaginary game. If . . . if he can beat the next car to the very next pole, then he'll become a president or a football star, he'll be tall and strong and have hair where he should, and rescue his mother from unhappiness. He runs, this boy, sprints hard, hears the exhaled roar of the approaching car, all certainty reduced to this yes-or-no test, given the clear resolution of a TV plot or a sports contest: if he wins, he gets what he wants, he'll be grown up, his future assured; if he loses . . . if he loses, he dies—the ultimate stakes in the game of life.

2

"We shouldn't have," S—— (Sonia? Sarah? Sally?) says, her voice soft, a sibilant whisper filigreed with guilt, her eyes averted and fixed on her drink. Watching her closely, B—— shifts in his seat, allows an appropriate pause before he speaks—like a priest, guilt's minion, professional absolver, he seems to know that rhythm and tone are as important as content.

"We couldn't help it; we couldn't help ourselves."

S—— nods, but it's a meaningless gesture, the vaguest acknowledgment of his presence there. "If only . . ." she says. Her voice drifts, her wishes die, reality emerges faintly as if

53

through tear-veiled eyes: a booth; a booth in a bar or a bar-restaurant; dark wood, dim light; a clock on the wall, some beer advertisement, says five after twelve, but is it day or night? Her hands, the pale and tentative tendrils of a vine seeking a solid base to secure its life or perhaps the carved praying pair of some bookend set, bracket her drink, fingers touching tip to tip.

"We shouldn't have," she says and bows her head.

The finality of it, the dead line, hope's evaporation, pain's circular ambit in her blue or emerald eyes. A myriad of possible paths to bring them here, the ever-forking trail of tragedy, but which is the one and what comes next? In the background, a fan's hum, its forced air rush, hot or cold depending on the season, ruffling the napkins beneath their drinks. B—— (Bob? Bart? Bertrand?) reaches out and touches the starkly venous surface of S——'s blue and white hand—compassionate, comforting, and cautiously watchful, alert for any subtle shift in mood.

"You mustn't blame yourself. You have feelings like anyone else. There was no resisting it for either of us."

S—— glances up; seems for a moment to grasp at that straw, food for her conscience. But a scrap for a starveling, it's not enough, and she bows her head again, letting it drop.

"I keep thinking," she says, "I keep thinking that there must have been a time . . ." She slows, pauses, allows herself a sigh; then spurts forward again only to die out a second time. "That there must have been a moment when we could have stopped, when we could have . . ."

S—— shakes her head; the room becomes clearer: a line of booths, each lit by a small wall lamp with an oiled-skin shade; a parallel bar with a fake brass railing; a few businessmen eating at a table; and in a distant corner, some blue-collar worker (a plumber, say, or a carpenter), drinking shots and beers in his company's overalls. Above him, a TV set is on, voices murmuring in watery color (a cop drama? a sports contest? a soap opera segment whose melodramatic dialogue will ironically frame the ensuing conversation between B—— and S——?)

S—— shakes her head; their strategies become clearer: hers, "*we must pay for what we do; I am responsible and, by implication, you*"; his, "*we are, all of us at times, prisoners of passion; we can't be held responsible where we had no freedom.*" The odds seems better that S—— is the one who has called the meeting.

"You know you're being too hard on yourself. These things do happen; it's not as disastrous as you seem to think."

There's no response; unassuaged, S—— stares at her drink.

"Life goes on," B—— continues, "we acted on what we felt; we were being human like anyone else." The clock's hands lurch forward, nine, then ten, then eleven after twelve, the potential of each moment relentlessly reduced. B—— calms, caresses, whispers, and soothes, tries to ease S——'s pain with the nepenthean phrases of his priestly brew. S—— raises her head and one can see now that her eyes are green, wreathes of withered fir on her face's snowbound field.

"We shouldn't have," she says.

The electrician in the corner laughs to himself; amber whiskey trembles in his glass. A bartender is created on the spur of the moment with a flushed forehead and a German accent. The paneling of the room is dark-stained oak.

"I just can't keep up a front. I can't go on living like this any more—the silence, the guilt." She waits; TV voices grow loud in the room, the circus barking of some game-type show; her alabaster hands wring the neck of her drink.

"I'll have to tell him," she says.

B—— (Billy? Barry? Burton?) straightens up; feels a trickle of fear as he imagines S——'s husband, some larvalike bureaucrat, turned wild-eyed and frothing, waving a gun he doesn't know how to use, demanding details he doesn't want to hear. A moment, just a moment of pleasure in picturing the scene, a sense of dominion and potency (he, *he* was the one to arouse all of this), but it's immediately overwhelmed by his loathing of complications, of needless pain and chaotic emotions—these self-inflicted crises.

"That won't do any good, you know."

He waits and then sighs, a sad bearer of sad tidings, when S—— grimaces, on the verge of tears.

"You'll only hurt him and hurt yourself."

She nods, then shakes her head, then nods again, her hand tossed into the air, a desultory pennant of despair and confusion. Slowly, she regains control of herself.

"It's Ricky," she finally says, "it's my boy I really worry about."

B—— squeezes her hand; the TV becomes clearer, its picture focused, the clarion call of its soliciting voices: a manic emcee and a vacuous model dangling prizes before a salivating crowd. "A bedroom set in maple veneer, a motor boat with fishing gear, a week's paid vacation to Las Vegas, Nevada . . . all this and more to today's lucky winner!"

B—— squeezes her hand; their strategies become clearer: hers, *"purge the guilt no matter what the cost"*; his, *"do not stir troubled waters."* Considering the kind of show and that the electrician is wearing his company's overalls, the odds seem greater that it's quarter after twelve in the afternoon.

"It's just . . ." S—— pauses, rearing her head as a round of wild applause emanates from the TV set. "It's just that he's at that age when life's confused enough as it is—sex and school and fighting with his father. He doesn't need this, her certainly doesn't need this hanging . . ." S—— shakes her head. "Myself, I don't care about anymore; my husband, he's not blameless, I know; but Ricky, if I hurt Ricky . . ."

She purses her lips, her pause replete with possible threats—murder or suicide or raging psychosis—and this additional guilt, a mother's potential betrayal of her child, overwhelms her at last, tears spilling from her evergreen eyes. Reaching into a nearby pocketbook, which might contain a vial of acid or pills or a loaded revolver, she retrieves a wad of Kleenex to stem the tide.

"But he doesn't have to know," B—— insists, "he doesn't have to be hurt at all." But then, hearing an edge of panic in his rising voice, he begins to calm down, refills the booth like an incense cloud with his softly plangent, liturgical balm: "Life goes on. We acted on what we felt. We did what was natural like anyone else. It was an act of love that neither of us could stop. There's no reason to go on punishing yourself. . . ."

The bald electrician tells a dirty joke. Hans, the bartender, has pomaceous cheeks and a Teutonic laugh. The ceiling of the room is lined with nets, its walls studded with nacreous shells and lacquered fish.

"There must have been a time," S—— begins to say (when she first caught his stare? when she told him her name? when he put his hand on her hip and she liked it there? Exactly when, exactly when did the possible become the real? Which moment was the last that she could have backed out?). "There had to be a point," S—— says half-aloud. "If only . . . if only," she says to herself.

A booth, a booth in a bar or a bar-restaurant. Horseshoe

crabs creep across the walls; grounded buoys and lobster pots guard the doors. In the corner, above the bar, a twenty-three-inch color television set is on, but no one seems to be watching it—not the table of men in suits and ties, not the man at the bar with "Evans Electronics" written on his back, not the thirtyish couple leaning forward in their booth, self-absorbed in their private world.

"I just can't take it," S—— says to B——, squeezing the dampened Kleenex in her fist. "I can't go on living a lie. I can't stand the way he looks at me now."

She pauses; the TV becomes clearer: an abrupt change in tone, grim revelations in a smooth baritone, some flash bulletin from the news department. (A kidnapping? a president's death? a grand tragedy ironically framing the smaller tragedy of B—— and S——?) S—— twists the Kleenex in her hand; the tragedy grows clearer, facts trickling in, the corpus delicti, the causal chain of infidelity:

"He never listens to what I say. Everything has to be done his way. And the money, the money he makes . . ." ("Ja, ja," Hans says again and again, pretending to listen to the bald electrician's drunken lament.) ("A mysterious explosion in mid-flight . . . all eighty-seven passengers presumed to be dead . . . a ball of crimson fire lighting the sky," the TV drones on, unattended.) "He doesn't care, he just doesn't care," S—— blurts out, both indignant and hurt. B—— nods his head; one of the businessmen laughs, bits of crabmeat salad, veins of pale green celery and pink orts of flesh, stuck between his teeth.

Calming herself, S—— bites her lip, rattles the ice of her vodka and tonic with a lemon twist. The clock, a plastic imitation of a pocket watch, with a beer's brand name instead of numbers on the dial, says twelve twenty-one. So much time elapsed, so many possibilities eliminated, and yet so many are left.

"Maybe I'll leave him," Susan says.

A pause. The words sink in. The walls are alive with lobsters and crabs, implications swimming in the silent air. Susan glances up. They exchange a stare, one long moment of communication, and their strategies are bared, reduced at last to irreducible meanings: hers, *"you got me into this, now get me out"*; his, *"we had one night and that's enough."*

"You shouldn't," B—— says.

He straightens up, his soothing voice lost, his hand receding like a retreating army as he reads the look in Susan's eyes. There, the plea has been transformed to a veiled demand, the tearful guilt to a subtle accusation aimed at him, an exacting of promises that were never made, that were not even implied—an imagined savior for her sorry life. This innocence, this helplessness, where were they the other night? Then, there had been no mention of a husband or son; then, another and less subtle demand had filled her eyes: she hadn't even wanted to finish her drink. *Women,* their sloughs of conscience, their nesting instincts, the invisible cocoon they perpetually spin, always trying to rope him in; the way they try to change the rules with their love of repercussions, these postcoital analyses and kaffee-klatsch guilt. And his predictable response, the expected claustrophobia descending on him now—to be free of this, to be back at work, to be sitting instead in his brother's house, relaxed and laughing at his brother's jokes . . . He had never, had never promised her anything more.

"I mean," Susan says, "what I mean is . . ."

The sound of change striking a table; a diver's helmet decorates a corner. Susan looks away, trying to reabsorb her em-

59

barrassing words, her clumsy angling to have him take her in. His panicky flinch, his eyes' mix of fear and disgust, are like a slap in the face. He seems so different to her now, suddenly pathetic, his beauty too posed and ridiculous, that silly phallic thing hanging around his neck the crudest form of caricature. God, the things he had done to her and she to him, the humiliating memory of what they had said, his compliments echoing back to her now like so many bad clichés from a thumb-worn script: just another trophy for his mantelpiece. And she had let herself hope that he would take her in! And she had let herself believe that he just might be the one to rescue her! If only she had had less to drink, if only she hadn't kept staring back at him, if only she had slapped that hand away from her trembling hip . . .

"I didn't mean . . ."

"I have to be free," B—— quickly fills in, all too aware of what she meant, his words expelled like a cloud of ink. "I'm not the kind of man who . . ."

"Ja, ja," Hans the bartender says, nodding his head; conch shells hang like rows of bombs from the ceiling's nets. A room, L-shaped, with a wooden door at either end and fifteen hundred square feet of space. Six booths, three tables, a twenty-foot bar with eleven stools, a black metal register with a bowl of lime green mints resting on it; above the bar, a seemingly inconsequential spider web which just might be a metaphor of the sexual war between man and woman. "Answer this question, Mrs. F——," the emcee says with melodramatic gravity, "and you'll be today's Grand Prize winner!" Six patrons and one bartender; two major characters and five minor ones; twenty-two minutes killed on the clock . . . just a few more left.

Susan swishes the dregs of her drink, the twist of lemon

awash in the vodka and ice like a mermaid's carcass on a jetty's rocks. Slightly ajar and leaning on its side, her pocketbook still lies nearby, still might hold a vial of acid or pills or a loaded revolver. Behind her, a door still exists which might still be an entrance for Susan's wild-eyed husband or for any of B——'s many past lovers. Murder or suicide or divorce or abortion, self-knowledge gained at the price of failure, the status quo rendered with ironic inflection, or any combination of the aforementioned . . . "Ja, ja," Hans the bartender says; he's heard it all again and again, the eternal lament, an age-old saga, more sad than tragic, of missed connections and long-lost love. The clock on the wall says twelve twenty-eight.

Susan and B—— slumped in their booth. A thirtyish couple apparently lost in their private worlds. Dark wood, dim light; beads of water condensing on their drinks. Neither one speaks. Pausing at the brink. The question of freedom in a relationship. Trying to chart an ending to this difficult scene, trying to choose from the many options left: for every word spoken, a million that aren't; for every life lived, an infinity that weren't; for every story's start, a hundred thousand different endings; for every move we choose to make, an endless wake of implications—and who is at fault? who is responsible? How does the real evolve from the possible?

"What I mean," Susan says; her hand drops to her drink, reassumes its old position, fingers touching tip to tip. Her voice fades; her gaze drops; she nods to herself, silent and sad, and the bar dissolving, a shroud enfolds her—the finality of her hopelessness. B—— is forgotten; dignity no longer matters; her own survival becomes inconsequential. She is alone now, alone with her guilt, sitting in a booth in a bar-restaurant, unaware that eighty-seven bodies, blazing like comets, have fallen from the sky, unaware that Mrs. F——, with a shudder and a scream and a buckling at the knees, has just been awarded the day's Grand Prize.

"It's my boy," she says at last; her lips, as blue as the veins in her hand, flutter as if mouthing a memorized prayer, her words so soft that B—— can barely hear them above the TV set. "It's Ricky I worry about."

3

Disoriented, Brad paused in the doorway, the air's web of cold mist a surprise, this outside world forgotten while sitting in the bar; and like some diver ascending in cautious stages, he stepped forward slowly, trying to spot his car in the vaporous lot, until, just a moment later, his bearings regained and suddenly anxious, he began to sprint, a suede jacket drawn over his head to protect his hair. Eyes to the ground, he watched the lot pass under him, a strange marshland mix of gravel and grass and oil-black mud, murky puddles strewn here and there like random hatches to an underworld sea. But once enclosed in the car, the terrain seemed ordinary again, the thud of his door a kind of italicized punctuation mark to his fear: over; finished; safe. Protected from the past and from the raw November air. Escaped. The familiar smell and feel of his car; the rain so soft that it made no sound; the traffic on the adjacent road swishing by in his mind like a caressing brush on a drum's tight skin. Escaped. Brad tried to smile, but the expression wouldn't work, no joy at all, not even the penumbra of relief. He glanced at the dashboard clock. "You'll be late back to work," he said to himself; then: "You're finished with her, thank God." But he didn't start the car.

Rapt and motionless, he stared straight ahead; intermittently, he would turn the windshield wipers on, erasing the mist with a few measured sweeps of the rubber blades. Captain Carl's Mariner Clam Bar would grow clearer then—its converted house front, its cedar shingles, a small sign adorning its roof with all the false modesty of suburban business: a parvenu disguised as landed gentry. Then, gradually, the view would blur again, droplets clinging to the glass like lint to felt, and he would flick the wipers on for two, quick, elucidating strokes. Susan didn't appear. Brad kept telling himself that she was probably having a second drink. Tufts of steam hovered above the hood of the car as if above a patch of moor, shifting gently with the wind. He glanced again at the dashboard clock, his eyes slowly drawn back to the entry of the bar: what was he waiting for?

This sudden dullness, inertia; this physical depression, an asexuality he wasn't accustomed to feeling. November with its menopausal grayness, desire dead and decomposing, the musty scent of rotting foliage. Neither chasing after nor eluding; no attraction, no revulsion . . . just sitting in the car. Brad opened the vent, a cool wet stream of air slipping in; he grabbed a cigarette and brought it to his lips: "You're finished with her, thank God." He was finished, all right, and now he had escaped, his freedom intact, just as he had—how many? twenty? thirty? forty times before? "I can't even name them all," Brad said to himself, but the words didn't have their intended effect; no excitement, no inflation, just another dreary fact of the dreary day—another dead leaf falling to the ground. The image arrested him; he watched as a single spent leaf descended before him, as faint as Susan's hand when, marbled with veins, it had collapsed to her drink at their meeting's end. Soundless, the leaf struck the ground; glancing down, Brad watched his own hand, a strangely distant, will-less object poised beside the ignition key . . . no, he couldn't even name them all.

Brad started the engine. Outside, touched by the lightly falling mist, the lot's weed-spiked puddles seemed to tremble; a lantern beside the bar door was on, the water-drenched air surrounding it atomized by light. Everything—the lot, the bar, his shifting thoughts—seemed to blend, suffused by a sadness immune to change, a namelessness. Brad reminded himself again that the after-lunch shift at work had begun, oscilloscopes methodically rolling off the line, no one there to test them out. A vision of his boss, furiously staring at a gold wristwatch, floated before him and then disappeared. Water slid down to the vent's chrome rim where, collecting at the tip, it dripped to his knee. Susan's stare, suddenly remembered—vacant and gray and cadaverously opaque above her drink—was cast upon the translucent windshield as if it were his own reflection, the haunting image of his present mood. Brad turned the wipers on, then off, tried to erase the image and the thought. (It wasn't his fault, after all; they both were adults, and he had his freedom to worry about; *he* owed nothing to her husband and son—she hadn't even mentioned them the night they had met . . .)

Brad waited; the doorway to the bar, though, remained empty, the wisps of fog encircling the car assuming the form of a premonition, bits of doubt coalescing into fear. As if about to step out, he reached for the door. A moment passed with his hand on the knob; but then, while he hesitated, a reflexive self-disgust suddenly embraced him, a sickening suspicion that he was being used. His hand clenched; turning abruptly on the seat, he stepped hard on the accelerator. The car lurched forward, spitting up gravel, skidding across the lot, past a poorly parked van with "Evans Electronics" stenciled on its side, and then onto the street where, straining against a hill, it rushed straight toward the slate gray void of the sky.

Utility poles; ranch houses; children dressed in yellow slickers; finely trimmed shrubs, suburbia's sculpture, crouching on lawns like tethered dogs . . . the hiss of water beneath his wheels. (Absurd, absurd, he couldn't be used; he'd been through these scenes too many times before, their master and manipulator.) The car slowed; trying to calm down, Brad turned on the radio, catching coverage of some plane disaster. A man at the airport was being interviewed; he had overslept the fatal flight and stunned by the miraculousness of his unearned luck, he rambled incoherently. "It makes you wonder," he kept repeating, and Brad, still talking to himself anyway (he had never, had never promised her anything more), turned the volume down.

Just beyond a school, the car evened out, drawing to a stop at an amber light on the top of the hill. There, mist still grew on the windshield's glass like teeming colonies of bacteria, and when Brad flicked the wipers on again, the view he gained startled him, as if this sudden sweep of clarity were some mental process, a burst of his consciousness piercing through reality's opiate veil. Alerted, he leaned forward, the glass already blurring before him. As far as he could see, embraced by the cold gray arm of the sky, stretched a valley of houses, suburban tracts of half-acre plots joined together like Siamese twins, freakishly identical: the town he had lived in most of his life. The same and yet different, set now in stark November, no sun to light the incessant white siding, leaves stripped from the trees whose darkly impoverished, reticulate branches were like cheap black stockings holding in place the town's adipose flesh. A woman, aging, her clothing torn off, her makeup smeared, her failing body's secrets unveiled—

varicosed streets, the stubbled hair of defoliated shrubbery, streaks of dead grass crossing the lawns like pale stretch marks on a middle-aged belly; a woman used, marked by time, a woman seen while saying goodbye in the morning-after's grimmest light: his dead affair's revulsion brought to life.

A sudden depression struck him—late for work, Susan's hopelessness, this suffocating domesticity all around him. The windshield blurred again, the radio's voice tapping on the fringes of his consciousness. Robotlike, he turned the wipers on and with the muffled pass of rubber over glass, the valley grew clearer, lot after lot of one-family houses, a patchwork quilt of pavement and grass and asphalted shingles. Their mazelike plenitude exhausted him, as if these neatly stacked boxes were so many oscilloscopes waiting to be tested, packages of womanhood demanding to be opened—a house on every lot, a woman in every house, and each one waiting for Brad's knock on her door, each one a challenge to his cunning and craftsmanship. Amazed, Brad said to himself, "This is what I do"; thirty down and a thousand to go; the factory's quota ever increasing, mass production's tedious accretion—all the punch-clock drudgery of his mission in life. Mist grew on the glass, slowly dulling his view just as familiarity dulled his desire for the women he knew. He flicked the switch again; his checkered hunting ground reappeared, its gnarled and naked trees, its mulch-clogged yards and misty streets, his own voice coming back to him now in an oddly hollow, haunting echo: "We couldn't help it; we couldn't help ourselves."

One moment after another, one woman then another, more drops of water collecting on the glass, house beside house in the suburban tracts; this endless cycle of desire and revulsion. "There was no resisting it." He couldn't help it, he couldn't help himself—as trapped as Susan. "I'm late for work," Brad said to himself, but he didn't move, on the verge, it seemed, of some sure conclusion, a reason for the day's despairing mood. The suspicion frightened him. His mind went blank. A long slow exhale condensed on the glass. He reached out eventually, rubbing the spot clean with his open palm, but by then, even with the wipers on, he couldn't see as clearly as he had before, reduced to the bell-jar space of his idling car.

The light changed; instinctively Brad shifted into gear, his car slowly drifting across the intersection. "It's not my fault," he said to himself, but he no longer knew for sure what he was talking about. A funeral home eased by, its professional greeter fastidiously British with top coat, hat, and black umbrella. A station wagon passed him on the right, children drawing faces on its clouded windows. Brad had left the wipers on, but the old clarity was gone, no insight now, his overview lost as the car descended the hill. His mind gone blank, only a feeling remained, a nagging uneasiness which seemed to pulse stronger with each stroke of the rubber blades, a sense of foreboding as though he were being drawn toward some awful conclusion against his will. A sputter of static caught his attention; panicking, he glanced toward the radio: the plane? was it the plane? did they say that the flight had been heading to L.A.? was his brother starting that California business trip today or tomorrow?

A southern drawl answered him, some syrupy pitch for country-style sausages. He reached out quickly, changing channels, desperate to find another news broadcast, unconsciously pressing the accelerator. The car gained speed, faster and faster, a water-spewing plummet into the maze of the valley: wilted grass, wisps of mist, a disintegrating leaf pressed against the glass, rows of picture windows with their drapes drawn tight, a porch-set pumpkin with a serrated smile . . . A car honked loudly, reminding Brad to keep to his lane; glancing up from the dash, he readjusted the steering wheel. (Absurd, absurd, he was sure that his brother was leaving tomorrow, sure that he wouldn't have changed his schedule; the odds against him being on that plane just had to be astronomical . . .)

But Brad didn't relax; he didn't ease his foot off the gas; and he didn't see the boy, R—— (Robert? Ronald? Ricky perhaps?), running hard beside him on the narrow sidewalk. Their race was foregone, a victory Brad was never conscious of—his sleek sedan, a silvery spray of mist and exhaust, still gaining momentum; the boy, weighed down by his rubbery raincoat, furiously pumping his arms and legs. R—— didn't give up. Brad never took his hand off the radio's knob. Locked into his car, his lane, anxiously listening to the radio's voice, he didn't see the boy's grimace of despair as the car whisked past him toward the finish line. And he didn't glimpse in the rear view mirror the stumble, the lurch, the limb-tossed collapse of the game's final verdict; never saw the boy's death-gasp shudder, a cold contraction to certainty, fluttering his raincoat on the puddled walk.

Alien Life

*O*UT OF THE NORTH, THEY MIGHT COME. OUT of Draco, guardian of the golden apples, that serpent stretching in a glissando of light notes across the sky; rushing out of Thuban, the old Pole Star, or from Rastaban or Eltamin, Draco's amber sleepless eye. Or from the south, out of Aquarius, a silver bead spilt from the cup of the Water-bearer; speeding past Sadalmelik, the lucky star, or from Sadalsund or Sadachbia, parting the luminous webs of the nebulae. Now or later, out of the past or out of the future, wiser than us beyond our knowing, they might come, colonies of consciousness, life that has spanned millennia of emptiness, riding the fluctuant waves of the space-time continuum. Through Cepheus or Cassiopeia, bearing messages or seeking refuge, escaping the catastrophic burst of a supernova: in the sky, a silent flash like a distant match and whole worlds are gone . . .

The buzzer rang. Unanticipated and loud, it bored through Bones like a morning alarm, a rude reminder of the mundane world; and jerking his head, he let the binoculars fall to his chest, his eyes called back from the measureless expanse of the star-studded sky to the cramped square formed by the tree house walls. The shift, that drastic reduction in his field of vision, enacted a kind of "quantum jump" in consciousness; he felt his mind condense from a numinous nebula of wonder and awe, a nameless timeless suffusion of stars, into a hard defined particle of self with precise coordinates in the here-and-now: the tree house, his backyard, 10:02 on a late March night. Zeroing in on the sound, he drew his attention to the table beside him. There, a light, of the sort that normally warned of machinery malfunctions like failing brakes or oilless engines, was flashing red, and turning on the chaise lounge, Bones stared through a spy-hole cut in the wall and across the lawn to his split-level house. At first, the scene was unclear; his eyes, still accustomed to the unaccountable depths of the moonless sky, needed time to resolve an image. But when they did and he finally spotted one of his daughters waving him in from behind the sliding glass door of their ground-level rec room, he cursed once under his breath and muttered to himself petulantly. *What could they want from him at this hour?*

His anger was short-lived. Even though conditions were ideal for observing, a rare conjunction of new moon, dry air, and near cloudlessness, he was vulnerable to more pressing responsibilities, ones he acknowledged willingly; and sighing, he supposed that the television had broken again or that Kit needed help with her algebra homework or, worse, that Mrs. Sweeney, Mary Beth's mother, had had another attack of senility and, mistaking their home for a hotel and Mary Beth for a presumptuous maid, she was demanding to speak to the manager—a part which, due mainly to the accident of his sex, Bones alone could play, convincing her to prolong her stay, "compliments of the management." And in any case, whatever its immediate cause, the interruption was, in part at least, Bones's fault too. He found himself a victim of his own cleverness and of his infatuation with gadgetry, an obsession so widespread among his neighbors that it seemed genetic, an expression of some definitive pattern within the species: des-

72

tined, it seemed, to reenact on a model-train scale, in basement workshops and makeshift attic laboratories, the technological wizardry that had conquered the planet.

"Why can't we just shout, like normal parents?" Mary Beth had asked, giving him that smile, both sarcastic and resigned, which captured the manifest paradox of her character—her devoutly Catholic cynicism.

She didn't understand, of course; the project wasn't hers, this tree house he was building for the kids, inspired by one of Kit's fickle wishes. She didn't understand the zeal behind his craftsmanship, his adamant insistence on "doing it right," the way he agonized over each decision with his minutely detailed analyses. Spy-holes in all four walls, a ceiling that could be raised by cranking a wheel, watertight joints and miniature furniture and two outlets for tensor lamps (no reading by flashlight necessary), the whole securely anchored to three low limbs of their backyard oak, but still high enough to provide a beautiful view: Bones had wanted to give his daughters a kind of magic kingdom, a place where they could feel both safe and isolated; and yet, too, at the same time, one from whose depths they could be conveniently called for bed or dinner. It was precisely this problem of "communication" that had worried Bones the most, and it was his worrying, overly grave for the situation, that had provoked Mary Beth's gentle mockery. But ignoring her, Bones had persisted, both with his plans and with his worrying; and in the end, secretly proud of the psychological subtlety behind his reasoning, he had chosen a simple buzzer and warning light, sensing that an intercom, which he had preferred at first (that engineering instinct asserting itself), would be too intrusive, alert to how the invasion of their parents' actual voices might destroy for the girls that atmosphere of sanctuary which was the special feature of a magic kingdom.

What Bones had failed to see, however, while engaged in all his well-intentioned analyses, was that the invasion had already taken place. His commitment to the project was an intrusion in itself, the house too "finished," too predefined to charm a child. Complete as a museum piece, it had no endearing weaknesses, nothing that might require compensating fantasies—and with them, the fanatical attachment of belief. It *was* beautiful, of course, and the girls *were* grateful when the hut had been finished five years ago. But their initial enthusiasm, even then more restrained than he'd anticipated, didn't last; and soon, like a Christmas toy long forgotten by Eastertime, the tree house joined a whole set of hobbies, friends, future careers whose attraction had proved no longer lived than their novelty and whose existence had now been overshadowed by the total eclipse of puberty.

Although keenly disappointed at first, Bones quickly understood. He saw, if too late, exactly how and why the project had failed; and when he would glance occasionally out their bedroom window and spot that product of all his ingenuity and love, perched as empty and forlorn as a deserted bird's nest atop the limbs of their backyard oak, the sadness he felt then was tempered always by a muted smile—the wry amusement of a man who, in middle age, has come to accept the foibles of his own character. So complete was his resignation that over a year had passed before he realized that the hut might be used as an observatory. It was an accidental discovery; trying to escape the range of Denise's stereo one night, he had simply retreated to the most distant point on their property. But once the connection had been made and he had spent an hour watching Saturn from within the tree hut's silent sanctuary, he couldn't quite shake its peculiar appeal. The wry smiles disappeared. He found himself leafing through old astronomy texts and paying attention to weather forecasts, returning to the hut with increasing frequency until, over a period of time, not unaware of the irony, Bones had made the tree house his own, adding key star maps and variable star charts to the walls, and stuffing the table drawer with soft cloths for cleaning lenses and with the wintergreen Lifesavers he habitually sucked in lieu of the cigarettes he had quit at the pleading of his daughters.

The ritual he followed rarely varied. On clear nights when it was possible, when there were no meetings to attend and no emergency household repairs to make, Bones would escape the house, climb the ladder, and ease himself through the narrow trap door which was the only entrance to his observatory. Then, safely inside, crouching within its child-sized space, he would crank open the roof until the sky was exposed and recline on an old chaise lounge he had wedged between the walls, staring upward. There was, often, a dizziness at first, a loss of bearings and security; he'd feel weightless for a moment, helplessly floating, as if he'd been spilled from the cradle of the Earth.

Hundreds of stars, crystalline points, would dazzle the eyes. A crescent moon might have cut a scythe of pale yellow light from the vault of the sky. Minutes would pass without event, the only sign of life the ghostly vapor of his shallow breaths, and all the while Bones would lie there waiting, for the slow adjustment of his nighttime senses, for his mind's surrender to the utter silence and open spaces. Patience was the key. There was no assurance just how long the process might take. But when the surrender finally came—that subtle release, that dissolution of self he cultivated—it was as if a second ceiling had been lifted, the dome to his inner observatory, and in those moments he became what he saw, drawn up and into that infinite expanse of punctuated light and depthless dark.

His binoculars, his telescope remained on the table. Later

he would focus on specific stars, read the charts, search the sky for distant comets—later he would become the amateur scientist. But at first he always watched like this, silent and still and instrumentless, luxuriating in a simple act of pure perception, in the incredible sensitivity of the dark-adapted eye. For these were the moments that kept bringing him back. Bones found himself moved in ways he couldn't express. The emotion he felt then, as he lay stretched between the tight cocoon of the tree house and the endlessness of the universe, seemed a strange mixture of yearning and contentment, as if he had been given the assurance of an answer and yet lacked the capacity to comprehend it, as if he'd been called by the Siren song of a distant star, drawn toward a beauty he could not reach.

The buzzer rang again, and again Bones flinched. Without intending to, he had slipped back into a passive watchful state of mind, mesmerized by the canopy of stars, and now, called back a second time, he stood up quickly, suddenly guilty, afraid that something might really be wrong. He didn't bother glancing back to the house; instead, he tilted the chaise lounge, raised the trap door, sliding through its narrow aperture. And then, in three long steps, his hands grasping rungs they had bought, cut, sanded, fit, he descended from the tree.

His feet struck the earth. Turning around, he surveyed the ground in all directions like a wary animal searching for predators, one hand still touching, as a child might the skirt of his mother, the coarse bark of the tree. Darkness had obscured the yard, giving an almost hallucinogenic twist to its familiar objects. The damp grass had acquired a pewter tint. Budded branches were transformed into a scourge of thorns raking the sky as they bent with the wind. A concrete birdbath, faintly luminous, sprouted from the grass like a mutant toadstool, some pale and poisonous A-bomb plant. The silence was complete, no foliage yet, no insects to busy the night with their manic cycles of life and death; and as Bones crossed the open yard, a vestigial fear as old as the caves hurried him along, past a coiled water hose, past a Frisbee and a rake and a bent garden trowel, past bags of charcoal briquets and fertilizer, all strewn about their barbecue grill—a "hearth scene" from which some future archaeologist might reconstruct their lives.

Relieved, allee-allee-in-free, Bones reached the patio, his wet sneakers staining its cement-set flagstone. Wolf packs, braking, froze on the grass. Saber-toothed tigers, afraid of the light, retreated limp-tailed to the fringes of the yard. Far above him in Ursa Minor, and on the still, silver surface of the birdbath's water, a single meteor announced itself, cut the lustrous streak of a prophecy no longer understood.

Bones pushed open the sliding glass door. "What's the matter?" he said as he broke through the drapes and into the room.

Anxious, his eyes blinked; the rec room was long, warm, brightly lit—free of any obvious emergencies. Denise, fifteen and an apparent victim of terminal ennui, lay sprawled on the couch, an open book, *Principles of Democracy,* tepeed atop her chest. On the floor below her, Kit sat transfixed, lacquering her toenails an opalescent pink.

"Telephone," she said without looking up, drawing a surgical line with the fine brush of the applicator.

"Telephone?"

Bones, suddenly annoyed again, glanced at his watch.

"Yes, Dad," Denise said languidly, "we've been meaning to talk to you about tying up the line with your calls every night."

Bones smiled in spite of himself and the girls began to laugh, Kit squealing with delight until she noticed that a droplet of polish, a trembling mercurial pearl of pink, had spilled from the brush and fallen on her knee. *"Shit,"* she said automatically; but then, remembering that her father was in the room, she winced, ducking her head, and cast a censoring hand across her lips—a series of gestures, however, caricatured embarrassment, which succeeded only in drawing more attention to herself. Bones, dazed, glanced away: the nail polish, the swearing, the styled hair were only three months old, and her abrupt transformation from tomboy to teaser, from baby-of-the-family to apprentice woman, still didn't seem real. After an awkward pause, he turned to Denise.

"Very funny," he said, and then, pointing to her book: "you have a test tomorrow, right?"

Denise groaned. Bones, after sneaking a glance at Kit again, climbed the stairs and headed down the hall, pausing, though, when through an open door he caught a glimpse of his mother-in-law.

Alone, Mrs. Sweeney sat against the dining room wall, rigid and pale, as proudly grave as a farmer's wife come to the city to beg money from a bank. With both arms she hugged her black leather pocketbook tightly to her chest, holding on as if it were a parachute pack whose contents could pillow somehow her plummet into death. *"My things,"* she called them—the family snapshots, the worn address book, the little gold pencil and religious medals, the nacre compact and bullets of lipstick—and the phrase, spoken with a gentle desperation, evoked the sad possessiveness of mummified pharoahs, clutching gold in their pyramidal chambers. Absurdly now, she wore a Sunday hat, festooned with lace, and a fur-trimmed coat which failed to hide the nightgown underneath, and Bones wondered as he waved a hello where she thought she was—at a bus stop? in a hotel lobby? in the hospital where she had waited for her husband for the very last time? In Einstein's universe, Bones suddenly remembered, his hand collapsing to his side, its greeting gone unrecognized, in Einstein's universe, time was just another dimension, preexistent, static like space, its intervals as simultaneous as a yardstick's marks. Even now, as her brain cells starved, somewhere in the space-time continuum, Margaret Sweeney was kissing the perfect fingers of her firstborn child. Even now as her body prepared for children of its own, in some nearby niche of the four-dimensional universe, Kit still cuddled on her father's lap, her whole being hung in the silken hammock of the stories he spun as their train rushed back from Newburyport.

Bones entered the kitchen. The clock on the wall said 10:07, and in that specific slice of the space-time continuum, Mary Beth sat at their kitchen table, assembling Easter baskets for St. Philomena's Home for the Aged. The stare they exchanged, when her dark green eyes slid in Bones's direction, was the rote, silent condensation of an argument they both knew by heart.

"He insisted," she finally said, turning back to her work.

"He?"

"A Mr. Turner."

"A *who?*"

Bones crossed the kitchen toward the living room phone, while Mary Beth put the final flourish on an Easter basket, curling the ends of its lavender bow. Shrugging, she said as he left the room: "He sounded like a Shakespearian undertaker." And in a delayed reaction, Bones didn't start laughing until he neared the phone.

"Hello?"

"Hello, is this Mr. Belmont?"

"Yes."

"Mr. Roger C. Belmont of 6 Berkeley Place?"

"Yes, I'm Roger Belmont."

"I hope I'm not disturbing you, Mr. Belmont."

"No," Bones said, lying politely, "no, that's all right."

"That's magnanimous of you, Mr. Belmont, that really is. You sounded as if you were having such a pleasant evening, and one hates to be a killjoy to conviviality. Perhaps you were socializing with some of your friends?"

Bones paused—*a killjoy to conviviality?* And yet despite the awkward formality and the forced attempt at an upper-class accent, the voice had a haunting quality, rich, deep, silkily soft; intimate, it purred with the gentleness of a lullaby, spiced though, too, with the subtlest shade of irony or sarcasm—just a hint of dissonance to complicate the tune. Blushing, Bones remembered suddenly how long it had taken him to return to the house and that he had been laughing softly when he had picked up the phone.

"I was in the backyard," he began, a vague apology meandering through his mind like a rivulet of rain lost in a field. "I was . . ."

"That's all right, Mr. Belmont. I'm accustomed to delays, I'm used to waiting, I accept the necessity of discipline and patience. And of course, if you're indisposed, I could always call some other night." He stopped, but the ending was false; a dramatic touch, a verbal trap. "Any night I choose," he said.

Surprised, Bones hesitated; the choice of pronouns seemed to negate the meaning of the offer, and the words, replayed, so soft still, so musical, danced in his mind with a teasing ambiguity. Frowning, he tried to identify the voice.

80

"Excuse me," he finally said, "but do I know you?"

"Oh, you know me."

"*Turner*—was that it? I'm sorry, but I just can't seem to place the name."

"Don't apologize, Mr. Belmont. We needn't bother with such inconsequentialities. What's a name, after all—a tab on a file? a quarter-cent label sewn on the soul? Immigrants had their names changed with the stroke of a pen. Slaves often had their names assigned."

There was a pause. Bones had the feeling that he was supposed to respond but, confused, he didn't know what to say. Silence, static-fringed, leaked from the phone; he considered hanging up, but then never moved, a growing fascination holding him in place. Even with its overtones of mockery, the voice had a strangely attractive aura of authority, seemed to beckon and soothe, to reassure Bones in some primal way; and he wondered suddenly, struck by what seemed an astonishing possibility, if this were the sort of voice—gentle and admonishing, supportive and mocking, all at the same time—which lured Mary Beth back to the confessional week after week.

"You didn't know that, did you?" the caller finally said. "You didn't know that slaves often had their names assigned."

"No," Bones answered obediently, "no, I didn't." And then, after hesitating: "But I do know you?"

There was another pause, time enough for the timid inflection, the little plea implicit in his question to echo in his mind pathetically. Glancing down, he noticed for the first time that the binoculars still dangled from his neck, and he saw then, trapped in the blue liquid pools of eyepiece glass, two tiny reflections of himself, the first step in some endless replication of the helplessness he felt, $2 \times 2 \times 2 \times 2 \ldots$

81

"Have you ever noticed, Mr. Belmont?" the caller said, and his voice seemed to luxuriate in the digression it made, testing, stretching, caressing each word, "have you ever noticed how the simple questions are often the most profound? Do you know me? Do I know you? Knowledge as a subject, an enigma in itself—what does the knower know when he knows? But then I shouldn't be wasting your time with these epistemological puzzles of mine, now should I, Mr. Belmont? I shouldn't try to impress an educated and enlightened citizen like yourself with my sophomoric philosophizing. It isn't my intention to bore you, Mr. Belmont—not after you've had the courtesy to speak to me at all. Not after you've had to come all the way from the backyard."

The caller drew a breath, seemed to reabsorb the mockery in his words, softening them again.

"So let's just get straight to the point, shall we? Let's just answer the question by saying that you know me *generically*, Mr. Belmont. Let's just say that you know my kind—you know the role I play in your life."

"Your kind?" Bones asked, but the truth was that he *did* know now what the caller meant, that he had discovered, without expecting to, a simple key to this strange event. For after peeling through the many layers of affect, the aural complexities of the caller's voice—the ornate and awkward formality, the baroque interplay of sarcasm and sympathy, the almost sensual richness of its timbre and tone—he had found at the core a single, blunt, infrangible fact: the man was black. A sliver of fear shot through him like shrapnel from a shell, a point of hot pain followed by a chill.

"I'm that dream you might have had," the caller said in a honeyed whisper (was he flaunting his blackness now, slurring the syllables, or was Bones just more aware of it?). "I'm that thought that crossed your mind as you waited alone for a bus one night. I'm that blur in the shadows, that noise in the dark, I'm that twinge that makes you sit up in bed or feel for your wallet when you're walking through a crowd. You know who I am, Roger, you know me all right. I don't even have to have a name of my own because *you've* already assigned me one."

"No," Bones said; but he was resisting the tone of gentle accusation without actually understanding what the accusation was.

"Come on now, Roger," the voice coaxed softly, "don't quit on me now, don't waste that arduous journey you made all the way from your backyard. You can tell me which one you like to use. When you're alone, when you're muttering to yourself as you watch the news, when you're laughing at jokes with your backyard friends. Nigger, is that the one? Spearchucker? Darkie? Sambo? Coon? . . ."

Bones listened, transfixed; the words flowed so softly into his ear, with such gentle encouragement and intimacy, that he might have mistaken them for terms of endearment, whispers across pillows in the middle of the night. But he had adjusted now, he had attuned himself to the hidden key, and just as his eyes, when accustomed to the dark, could extract from the sky teeming colonies of individuated stars, so could Bones hear now in the velvet void of the caller's voice the subtle song of hate which was meant for him alone.

He didn't want to believe it. The sheer malevolence, the fixed intent to terrorize, amazed him; and looking up, he glanced around his living room, with its colonial furniture and family pictures and blue medallion wallpaper, trying to draw some hidden connection between this modest, tranquil, familiar setting and the disembodied venom seeping slowly in his ear. But there was none and he knew it; he knew suddenly and with absolute surety that the caller was a stranger, that his was a missile shot off at random, that any one of a thousand numbers might have been called instead. Strangely, though, there was no comfort in that fact; it only made his sense of injustice seem irrelevant, left him there like a stunned pedestrian protesting his innocence to an oncoming car. And he was struck then, a rush of strangeness lightening his head as if all the rules of order had been bled away, by the improbability of his own existence: the unlikelihood of having been called, of having bought this house, of having married Mary Beth or found his job, the unlikelihood of being alive at all. A million to one, a million million million to one; all the sperm spilled, all the stars that filled the cobalt bowl of the sky—and how many bore life?

Bones blinked; the room, frail and unreal, seemed to shimmy, dissolve, fold in on itself. And closing his eyes, he visualized then his tormentor's finger, its blackness, its knuckles and nails, the pale rose of its palm-side skin; imagined the parabolic curve of its rise and fall, and how, as thoughtless as hail, it must have struck ("chosen"?) a single line on a printed page: Roger C. Belmont, 6 Berkeley Place. That was all it took, an arrow of chance, to actualize this point in time and space. That was all it took to focus and unleash, to make Bones the target of all this hate.

Suddenly Bones remembered Emily, and the image of her, rising in his mind, so startled him that he didn't hang up the phone as he'd intended. He remembered her hair and the way its auburn bangs had bounced and splayed as she had whipped her head in his direction. He remembered her hand, the way it had leaped defensively, its pearl ring blinking at him, drawing attention to her high-set breasts. He remembered clearest of all her frozen stare of fear and surprise, the slackened lips, the wide brown eyes, the way she seemed to hold her breath and then, more vulnerable still, surrender it, her silence timed to the thud-thud of the duplicator as they stood there alone in the office basement. And the amazement he had felt then, with the unfolding recognition of what her reaction meant, seemed a secret link to the present moment and to that voice of malice humming softly in his ear.

She was young, twenty-three then, twenty-four—"intern" was the term the company used as if, by evoking the medical profession, it could infuse its M.B.A. and law school recruits with the true gravity of their corporate mission. She was young, nervous, quietly ambitious and, given the omnipresent cowardice which passed for cleverness in their firm, the constant measuring of each new employee as a potential threat to one's own career, she was left to struggle on her own. That he had come to her aid on her very first day was accidental. He had been walking by, saw the files piled on her desk, and realizing that the figures she was so desperately trying to compute could be obtained by a simple call to the research department, he had done nothing more gallant than telling her so. Afterward, it was true, Emily had come to him frequently to ask for help, but that, too, was hardly abnormal—all the interns did. His name, he had always supposed, was shared between them like some fraternity password, a final bequeathing to the incoming class: "Belmont's the one who'll save your ass."

It wasn't a crusade. His generosity was more reflexive than principled and arose in part at least from his complete indifference to the corporate game. Bones knew that he did his job well, but he knew too, given his attitude, his inability—congenital, it seemed—to take the business seriously, that he

85

would rise no further in the hierarchy; and it was this sure knowledge which allowed him a freedom the ambitious didn't dare. The freedom to relax. The freedom to answer a question if someone asked without calculating first its eventual effects.

It was an aloof sort of kindness and never naive; he knew to expect little in return for the many favors he did. And it was precisely because he took such pride in this, his realistic view of office life, that Bones faulted himself now for failing to detect the problem sooner than he had. For Emily had been different from the start. Unlike the other interns who, afraid to be seen as dependent or weak, often tried to dismiss the assistance they'd received, even to themselves, she acknowledged his help in any way she could. She might pick up his mail or run his papers down to the duplicating room; she might remind him of a meeting or leave a piece of homemade fudge lying on his desk. Nothing was ever said. She was just as shy as she was painfully determined to succeed at her job, and Bones, compliant as always, followed her lead. The truth was that he wasn't paying much attention to the subject. If he thought about it at all, he did find himself "touched" by these wordless displays of gratitude, but touched in the way he found his daughters touching, when, both amused and saddened by them, he observed some trait, like the way Kit used to clutch the seam of his pants, that would never survive their growing up.

But then, there came the president's monthly seminar and Emily's attempt to rescue him, and Bones was finally forced to see what his nonchalance had hidden from him.

Grasping the phone, only subliminally aware of the caller's voice, Bones blushed even now when he recalled his performance that afternoon. Careful planning couldn't have arranged a better forum for his humiliation; for occurring on the last Friday of every month, the "seminars" were just the sort of program meant, along with community blood drives and public television sponsorships, to evince the enlightened nature of the management. Lunchtimes on these predesignated days were extended an hour. During this interval the employees would gather in the auditorium to hear a talk given by one of their own: a talk, lecture, slide show, or performance even—Ms. Cohen of Accounting riding the keys of a Chopin piece as if it were a bucking bronco. The vision, as conceived by the personnel office or the president's wife, no one was sure which, radiated a certain fifteenth-century atmosphere: the modern corporation as Italian city-state; its president a de Medici, its staff a cast of devoted artisans creating for posterity, its home office a Florentine palace alit with a rainbow array of Renaissance talent. "Diversity" was the theme in this "celebration of our gifted employees" (phrases snatched from a descriptive paragraph in the annual report to the stockholders). And the only rule enforced was that the subject *must not* relate directly to the company's business, thus offering, like a wedge of exposed thigh, the secret thrill of irrelevance to a corps of junior executives who were afraid to discuss even sports without engrafting it first into the metaphorical realm of the corporation.

Like most charitable gestures conceived from above, the program was despised by those it was supposed to benefit. It was, nevertheless, something of a perverse success; indispensible to office morale in a way never envisioned by Personnel. For the seminars were the only regular occasion when a staff normally rent with mistrust and dissension found themselves united behind a common cause. One day a month, they communed in their contempt, shared the sarcasm of the oppressed; and the attitude which bound them up was best expressed by the name they'd given to this "celebration" of themselves forced upon them by the management. "Show and Tell," they called it.

When Bones's turn came to "show and tell," the topic he chose was extraterrestrial intelligence. That was his first mistake, he realized now; not because the subject was too foolish or exotic—that hardly seemed possible in a program that had seen Mr. Cassin's beer can collection and Mrs. Beck dressed in a geisha costume—but simply because it mattered to him. His love of the stars, his lifelong addiction to science fiction had both been born in part from a boyhood fascination with alien life, and that fascination, the lure of an alternative intelligence, an entirely "other" way of being, had never really died. It was, in a way, Bones's only belief, the last dim candle flame of faith in the fact-lit world of his ordinary life. He embraced it in the way Mary Beth seemed to embrace her Catholicism, not with a fanatic's insistence but with a wry surrender, a timid bow to hope. Somewhere up there in the spectacular heavens there just might be a creature who had surpassed our limits, who had escaped the ache and despair, the constant confusion, who knew and might supply the secret ingredient missing from our lives which would make us happy.

Bones didn't insist; he didn't believe in UFO sightings or expect an alien landing by the end of the decade. The possibility alone was enough, the chance, as confirmed by serious scientists, that we were not alone in the universe. The slim chance that they might come to us.

Bones closed his eyes again. The caller's whisper, with its soliloquy of insinuation, still hummed in his ear and yet he didn't listen, focusing instead on the day of his presentation, and how, cocky before the fall, he had even begun to enjoy himself, posturing there behind the lectern. He had known the material well. There was a microphone so that he didn't have to worry about the strength of his voice. He even sensed some interest in the audience, although he was careful not to study their faces, afraid to catch the eye of the president who always sat in the rear like some Speech-and-Drama teacher grading his pupils on their elocution. It was only at the end, after presenting the subject so objectively that it was impossible to deduce what his own views were, that he began to lose control of himself. Asked what extraterrestrials might be like if they did exist, he was about to answer, when someone in the audience blurted out:

"Cybernetic!"

Startled, Bones scanned the seats below him, but the comment, both its content and its rudeness, had already hinted at who the speaker was. It had to be LaMonte, their brilliant but arrogant computer specialist, whose habit of interrupting conversations with his inflexible opinions had arisen, Bones assumed, from a lifetime of prodigious classroom performances—always barking out answers to blackboard problems a step ahead of the other students. Sadly, he never seemed to have learned that his authority might not extend beyond the limited range of his mathematical gift.

"What's that?" Bones said. His tone was polite, but he was secretly annoyed at the interruption and snuck a nervous glance at his watch on the lectern.

"Advanced, self-programming, self-replicating computers," LaMonte replied with disdainful brevity—apparently verbs weren't necessary when you knew the answers.

Bones spotted him in the audience. With his chaotic hair and horn-rimmed glasses and a tie that scissored down his shirt like the thin legs of a draftsman's compass, he looked so much the caricature of the abstracted, bloodless scientist that it seemed self-conscious—as if, accused all his life of having a computer for a heart, he had rebelled finally by embracing the charge, trimmings and all.

Bones, trying to avoid trouble, nodded vaguely in LaMonte's direction, the sort of strategic nod given to babbling children and ranting madmen, and then returned his gaze to the original questioner.

"The point is," he said to Freeman of Sales, "that we have no way of knowing what they would be like. The point is that they're apt to be so different from us that they're actually beyond our imagining."

"The point is," LaMonte mimicked disdainfully, "that no crude living creature could survive the trip. *The point is* that in a civilization that advanced, computers would be the ruling force."

"Nonsense," Bones snapped; fiddling with note cards, he tried to calm himself, tried to douse the flames of flushed heat he felt streaking up his neck. But there was something about LaMonte that infuriated him; something about his demented seriousness, his groundless arrogance, the squandering of his talent on gimcrack projects, that reminded Bones of the company itself. All that was missing was the smooth facade, the patina of P.R. charm.

As if reading from a chart, LaMonte was listing aloud the distance in parsecs to the nearest stars when Bones interrupted him.

"So extraterrestrials, if they exist, if they arrive here at all, will have to be machines—is that it?"

"Advanced, self-programming, self-replicating computers," LaMonte insisted, an exact repetition; the answer, once computed, could not vary.

"Why?" Bones said, and as he watched LaMonte's contemptuous sneer, he felt the heat rise from his neck to his cheeks. "Why would they come?" He hesitated, but LaMonte, silently superior, still refused to speak. "What possible purpose would a machine have to make such an epic journey across the universe? There would have to be a motive, LaMonte; there would have to be an emotion. These machines of yours, these advanced, self-programming, self-replicating computers, would have to feel something strongly to undertake such a mission—and machines don't feel."

Bones paused again; he was vaguely aware that the audience had begun to stir in their seats, vaguely aware that his voice had changed, tighter, high-pitched, faintly hysterical. But all he could see was LaMonte, with his ridiculous tie and arrogant smirk, the way he straightened his posture as if to align himself with some invisible doctrine whose manifest truth could never be doubted. And for an instant, as he watched LaMonte resist speaking, Bones was reminded then of Mrs. Sweeney and the way, like some statuary saint secure in her niche, she used to freeze, deaf, whenever someone attacked the Church.

"Why?" he finally said again, bearing in, pointing at LaMonte with the note cards he had crushed in his hand. "Why would they even make the trip?"

LaMonte blinked back at him stubbornly. "Why would anyone?" he said.

Bones dropped his hand. A bubble seemed to have burst, his encapsulating anger instantly gone, pricked by a question which, although long considered, he still couldn't answer. And without an answer or his anger, no longer obsessed by LaMonte's behavior, Bones suddenly became conscious of the audience again, its many faces, the president lurking somewhere in the distance, his watch ticking off time on the lectern before him. The phrase *"Show and Tell"* shot through his mind, ribboned with scorn, followed then by the panicky thought, *I'm making a fool out of myself.* He realized that the silence had gone on too long, but riveted in place, his mouth as dry as the cloth of his suit, he couldn't say a word. It was then, a miracle when he so desperately needed one, that he heard Emily's voice.

"Mr. Belmont?"

Relieved, Bones focused on her, reduced the anonymous and suddenly terrifying audience to a single face whose timid features he was accustomed to. Emily was blushing, her voice so soft that he could scarcely hear her, but he understood immediately that she was trying to help him, giving him a chance through the simple questions she asked to recover his composure.

Back in the office after the talk had ended, after he had received an applause whose enthusiasm had seemed surprisingly genuine, Bones had not at first, beyond the dumb fact of his gratitude, considered Emily's action. He was too relieved, and too furious with himself for having risked his carefully wrought immunity, to recall how shy she normally was, how reluctant to speak in front of groups; too stunned still to ask himself what it must have been that had driven her so far beyond the orbit of her cautious personality. But then, at the end of the day, he had descended alone to the duplicating room, accidentally surprising her there. And caught off guard, she had revealed herself, she had . . .

"Roger?" the voice said; and Bones, stirring, glanced at the phone in his hand, felt himself slide between separate realities, between his living room with its wingback chairs and the caller with his soft malicious intimacy and that moment, two years ago now, when he had blundered into the duplicating room. In the pause where those three worlds met, he could almost hear the thundering heartbeat of the copying machines as they did their work.

"Roger C. Belmont of 6 Berkeley Place?"

"Yes," Bones said. But even as he spoke he was seeing Emily again, reading that unexpected expression that had wounded her face—the frozen stare of fear and surprise, the slackened lips and wide brown eyes.

"You're tuning out on me, Roger, you're absconding again to your backyard. I'm aware that I may be boring you, I'm cognizant of the fact that I have a tendency to excessive verbiage; but an enlightened citizen such as yourself will understand that a man like me can't help himself. You know how a nigger will talk."

Bones stared at the blue medallion wallpaper; the phrase "excessive verbiage" floated in his mind like some odd and faintly noxious fragrance. As he closed his eyes, Emily again appeared in his mind, her hand sinking, its pearl ring shimmering, her breath released as she slumped in surrender. She had waited there like docile prey, all her little acts of gratitude, all her shy silences and her heroic rescue, suddenly framed, explained by this moment of vulnerability. It had come to him with perfect clarity, startling and yet with a dream's timelessness and subtlety: there was only one way to read that stare, just one possible cause behind its tortured blend of longing, fear, hope, and pain.

"*Roger,*" the caller snapped; he was losing his patience now and with it, his soft intimate assassin's whisper. "You *listen* to me, Roger C. Belmont of 6 Berkeley Place!"

Bones drew in a breath, more amazed than frightened by the focused fury of the caller's voice—amazed, as he had been that day in the office basement, that he could be the target of so much passion; amazed and ashamed, terribly ashamed, that all he felt in return was a dazed detachment. She had waited there like docile prey, she had stared at him and her stare had been a plea, a question . . .

"You better listen up, you better not dare tune out on me! But then, you're that kind, aren't you, Roger—you're just that sort of chickenshit suburban cracker. You're the one who always thinks he's escaped, who always thinks he's safe in his little backyard. You're the one who always thinks he can hide behind a liberal smile the disgust he feels for niggers like myself."

There was a moment's pause, the caller trying to calm himself (the room, Bones suddenly remembered as if smelling it now, had reeked of ink); his final words, whispered again, were hoarse with hate.

"You're the one, aren't you, honkie?"

Bones pulled the phone away from his face, stared into the holes of its plastic mouthpiece. All the other numbers in the book, all the other men who might have loved her in return, and yet *he* had been picked—she had never taken her eyes off him.

"No," Bones said, shaking his head. "No, I'm not."

Slowly he hung up the phone; slowly he had turned from Emily and left the room, his memo, uncopied, still clutched in his hand. After taking a few steps across the living room rug, he stopped, hesitated, and then, bending down, unplugged the cord to the telephone before he entered the kitchen again.

There, surrounded by jelly-bean bags and marshmallow chicks and gold foil-wrapped chocolate eggs, Mary Beth was assembling her Easter baskets, a one-woman charity factory. Anxious for company and yet unable to talk, Bones leaned against the counter and watched her work.

94

"Who was it?" she finally asked, without looking up.

"Just a crank." But in the silence that followed he heard once more the purring malice of the caller's voice. He pushed forward; the man *hated* me! he wanted to tell her, all his amazement rising again. But then, shaming him, he remembered Emily, and how she had stood, forsaken, before the copying machines, and sagging, he dropped back against the counter again.

"That figures." Using both hands, she fluffed a nest of cellophane shreds. "Sorry," she said.

Bones nodded, but she wasn't watching him. A moment passed. "Finished soon?" he finally asked her.

"A few more to go." Grabbing a chick, she set it in a basket, rearranged it, and then, tilting her head, attempted to gauge the artistic affect. "You going back out?"

"I guess . . . for a little while." And then, absurdly, as if he needed an excuse: "I left the roof up."

There was a long pause, but Bones still didn't move; guilty without cause, he felt a frustrating urge to confess, converse, to explain himself. Anxious to finish, busy assembling baskets whose carefully considered aesthetic arrangements would soon be razed by the chocolate-crazed ladies at St. Philomena's, Mary Beth scarcely acknowledged his presence. Eventually, when he heard in the distance the murmuring voice of their TV set, he pushed away from the counter, squeezed her lightly on the shoulder, and left the room.

Bones headed for the stairs; he paused, though, when out of the corner of his eye he spotted Mrs. Sweeney again. Sitting in the same chair, she hadn't moved an inch, frozen like a spider at the center of her diminishing web: her fur-trimmed coat an artifact; her nightgown, off-white and ankle-length, dangling below it like an errant slip; her cache of "things" still hugged hard with both arms, drawn in like a gasp, hoarded breath, toward her center space. Her bus hadn't come in, or the doctor arrived yet, bearing bad news from the operating room.

"Hi, Mom," Bones said, taking a step in. A slight shift of her head was the only response, her thick glasses casting back planes of reflected light like mica scales set in rock. A moment later, one of her calcified hands slid over an inch, guarding the latch of her pocketbook, and that pathetically slow reflex of blind mistrust triggered in Bones a surge of feeling. Its strength surprised him; tears dampened his eyes. He had never much liked her and that somehow made his sympathy now seem more genuine, more profound, beyond himself; pure like the stars. Mary Beth might someday sit like this, he suddenly knew—Emily too. The sadness deepened, seeped through his body like sinking water, a percolating ache, a form of exhaustion; the image of Emily, her auburn hair turned thin and gray, her young and painfully hopeful features mineralized into senile suspicion, offended him and yet left him helpless. There ought to be something more than this, there ought to be more—somewhere, somewhere in the space-time continuum . . .

"Beautiful night, Mom," Bones said, backing away, a smile (for whom?), idiotic with cheer, fading from his face. People talked to plants like this, hoping they would grow.

Silently Bones descended the stairs. Below him Denise still lay on the couch, *The Principles of Democracy* still weighing her down as if graved in stone like the Ten Commandments; while Kit, her beautification finished, each toe tipped a pearly pink, lay sprawled on the floor, a child again, her hair loose, her legs cast out carelessly. And with the moving images on the TV screen holding their attention like dancing flames in a

fireplace, their expressions passive, unguarded, blandly con-
tented, they seemed to Bones too vulnerable, utterly exposed
even here in their home, this split-level house he had bought,
rebuilt, tended for them with the specific intention of keeping
them safe. Never before had he been so aware of all the many
things he couldn't protect them from, the suffering which
would be their inheritance just as surely as binocular vision
and the opposable thumb. Like Mrs. Sweeney; like Emily; like
all the failure-fearing interns who snuck into his office; like
the widowed ladies at St. Philomena's, counting off beads
while they waited for their candy. Even LaMonte was
not immune, cybernetic LaMonte who pretended to prefer
machines to people; even he was afraid to die, wanted a
love he couldn't find, hid behind his disdainful smile a baf-
fled panic, a nervous blink of incomprehension. Humans,
men and women, not advanced, self-programming, self-replicating computers. Born, it seemed, with something missing.
Stranded here without an answer.

Bones reached the bottom of the stairs. Fear triggering fear
as he watched his daughters, he suddenly remembered the call
again.

"You know," he said, drawing close to the couch; pausing,
he glanced away and cleared his throat. It was strange the way
his love for them could render him stuttering and shy, like
those adolescent boys calling Denise now who whinnied in
panic, their voices sliding up and down in search of a confi-
dent register, whenever he or Mary Beth answered the phone.
"You know that you shouldn't . . . I mean, if a stranger ever
came up to you . . ."

In unified dismay, the girls turned their heads toward him.
He glanced down, aware of what a ridiculous figure he cut,
with his binoculars and his old college sweatshirt, its sleeves

97

torn and shrunk, and with BONES, his fraternity nickname (only Mary Beth still called him that, and then only in bed), stamped in fading letters across the front. As if he hadn't changed his clothes, or the opinions he held, since the homecoming game in '61.

"You know that if a strange man . . ."

"Father," Kit squirmed, embarrassed for him. Denise rolled her eyes, world-weary and impatient: another lecture from the old man, #12 A, cross-referenced under *drugs, sex,* and *kidnapping,* entitled "Beware Strange Men and Candy-Bearers." And yet Bones persisted, risked the caricature—he had his responsibilities.

"Well?"

"Yes, Dad," Denise said tolerantly; she had already turned back to the television program.

"Kit?"

A single nod, Kit's ten pink toes, like a blushing crowd, trying to hide themselves in the shag of the rug, and his mission was accomplished. Moments passed. As if trying to pretend the conversation hadn't taken place, all three of them stared silently at the TV set. Bones, noticing then that the images on the screen had a wan, blurred, almost subaqueous cast, made a mental note that he would have to adjust the color again.

The prospect wearied him; he let out a sigh—the moribund hiss of a punctured tire. Another "thing-to-do" on his household list, another repetitious task which seemed to him then to evoke, embody all the other tedious tasks that, bit by bit, consumed his time—cleaning the gutters, changing washers, rising for work at 7:05 every weekday morning. Helpless, he began to tick them off, the relentless steps, the serried spokes of the spinning wheel which was his life, round and round.

The same commute, the same morning agenda, the same calls, the same meetings, the same lunch at 12:45, the same "generous" extension once each month for another ludicrous round of Show and Tell. In July, with the regularity of a migrating bird, a new intern would arrive, and soon, given the secret word, would seek Bones out, his eyes blinking the same SOS above the same nervous ingratiating smile. Even the consolations of home seemed suddenly pale, his marriage too harried, too habit-bound, his daughters slipping away from him now, outgrowing this nest just as they'd outgrown the play-house he had built in their backyard oak five years before. Magic kingdoms didn't last—nor did their cherished inhabitants.

Bones sighed again. He seemed unable to move; stared dully at the screen as if, instead of the facile sit-com unfolding there, he were watching some televised version of his own existence, protesting now without hope of redress the mundane plot, the endless commercials, the lack of originality: why should he have to live a life like this? . . . why should anyone?

Remembering the phone call then, Bones began to feel for the first time the resentment, the outrage which the caller had meant to arouse in him. He had been fine, he had been completely content watching the stars on a lovely night, when the call had come in, reminding him of Emily and of his daughters' vulnerability, filling him now with this dull discontent. His anger, though, didn't last. It couldn't survive his memory of, what seemed to him now in retrospect, the almost comic delivery of the terrorist, with his histrionic whisper and awkward formality, his pretentious imitation of an avenging angel: a "Shakespearian undertaker"—Mary Beth, as usual, had captured it perfectly, unmasked him from the start. And for a moment then, as he tried to imagine the caller's life (he would have a dim monk-cell room, its walls cluttered with newspaper clippings justifying his hatred and with vocabulary words which he loaded into his mind like machine-gun shells awaiting a target; there would be a plain black phone, surrounded by the crumpled wrappings of franchise food, and a limp telephone book, its columns smudged with fingerprints), Bones almost envied him; envied his mad commitment, his sense of purpose, of mission, the glorious delusion he must have held that these murderous phone calls made a difference. Again he felt an amazement rise; the style had been affected, but not the message it bore or the feeling behind it. The man's hate had been real, as real as the innocence Bones had felt in return, as real as the courage Emily had shown on the day of the monthly seminar. Bones's mind swirled with comparisons, a superluminal shuttle between realities, a vision of the avenger's stabbing finger giving way to the slow collapse of Emily's hand, evoking the thud-thud of the duplicating room with its windowless walls and stench of ink, which, in another spin of the wheel, another quantum jump return to the here-and-now, became the pungent scent of nail polish fanned throughout the room by Kit's wriggling toes.

Bones stared at the TV screen; nothing had changed during his imaginary journey through time and space: the same characters trapped in the same situations; the same watery colors which would have to be adjusted.

"I left the roof up," he said to himself, a dazed prod, an excuse to move; and then, as if still conversing with Mary Beth: "I guess I'll go back out for a little while." The command, as though beamed from a source in distant space, took an extra moment to reach his legs. Slowly he turned; mechanically he crossed the room and slid open the door. As he took a step outside, a burst of canned laughter, erupting on cue from the TV set, followed him onto the patio—another joke on the hapless hero.

The door slid shut, sealing him off; seemed to suck the laughter away from him, leaving him alone on the patio in its dim sphere of borrowed light. Kit's faint silhouette, as if waving goodbye, swayed with the pleated drapes on the other side. His own shadow lay at his feet, larva-shaped, like an idea of himself not yet complete, an evolutionary hypothesis. The wind, seeping through his clothes, chilled his back, and standing there, motionless, he absorbed the cold, recharging himself, making a slow return to consciousness.

Shivering, Bones turned. At the rear of the darkened yard, the tree house waited—square, white, slightly luminous; a bastion of ghostly logic amid the twisted chaos of the oak's bared limbs. Drawn to it, he began to walk, the path he had taken so many nights before, across the flagstone patio, between cinder-block walls topped with dying geraniums, past a rake, a Frisbee, a domed barbecue grill, past bags of briquets and fertilizer—all the civilizing tools of suburbia. The withered hand of a garden trowel reached up from the ground; a green water hose lay curled like a sleeping snake in the middle of the lawn. Bones felt a little leap, a quickening inside, when his feet sank into the deeper grass, a primitive fear like some fetal form of life stirring itself—blind, wriggling, insatiable— in the depths of his mind: there was danger out there in the dark; serpents, wolf packs, saber-toothed tigers, black men bent on avenging injustice, lurking somewhere on the fringes of the yard.

Bones began to run, slowly at first, but then faster and faster, a confused excitement urging him forward. Away from the house, the phone, away from his wife, his daughters, his mother-in-law, across the pewter-tinted lawn toward the furthest darkest reaches of the yard. The binoculars bounced against his chest; his own hunched image startled him as it slid across the birdbath's surface; the tree loomed close, an ancient home, the ladder hung like some varnished rule measuring in rungs degrees of escape. He leaped up, skipping a step, his hands locked into a power grip, pulling him up and away, through the narrow entry, and then onto the floor of the observatory. There, winded, he caught his breath. A minute passed while he stared, uncomprehending, at the muddle of grids and points which crowded the star charts tacked to the walls. In a series of rote steps, he closed the trap door, lowered the chaise lounge, turned away from the house, and then, collapsing backward, he closed his eyes and laid himself down.

When he gazed up at first, the sky seemed to spin, a whirlpool of stars, a dizzy fractured wheel of chance. He blinked; his heart beat fast; he fidgeted, squirmed, anxious again, finally turning away, glancing first at the red warning light, and then, not trusting it, through the spy-hole he had cut in the wall behind him. His home, though, seemed safe—silent, haloed in light, protected by its moat of grass and shrubs. Calmer, he shifted again, settling in, sinking into the loosened webbing of the chair, into the quiet, the cold, the clear March air. A single cloud, translucent doubt, slipped away. As if the finest veils were being peeled from his eyes, the stars grew clearer, hard-edged, crystalline. A great longing began to fill him, lured by some promise he sensed within the endless depths of expanding beauty: all the numberless worlds, each a possible home; all the focused flames of hope populating the void . . . Thuban, the old Pole Star; Rastaban or Eltamin . . .

Bones drifted. Another cloud passed, blown by the wind.

Effortlessly the last veil lifted, that dome to his inner observatory, and he forgot the facts, the charts, forgot who he was
and what he wanted to ask; surrendered a breath and, escaping
with it, hovered midway between the earth and the stars. And
there, alone, he waited for them to come, with their whispers
of hate, with their stunned stares of love.

The Death of Descartes

HOUSE ON THE NORTHERN COAST OF Maine. One story high, its rectangular sections extend in three directions, fitting through the abrupt rise and fall of the promontory rock: prosthetic limbs, mechanical fingers, angle-jointed, clinging there against the wind like the roots of a scrub pine. Easy to frame, and in fact frames itself with an encircling metallic railing, a futuristic boardwalk which flirts with the cliff's uneven edge and overlooks the cove. Two materials dominate—steel and glass. One color—orange. Five hundred feet below, the North Atlantic, a white-capped winter ocean, its dull green brine squeezing like a spittle-tipped tongue into this gouge in the highlands, and interrupted only by jutting thumbs of tide-sculpted rock. Clouds, gray-bellied, blur the gulls. No other life. A few pine trunks, polished of their bark, tucked at gravity-defying angles into the cliffside notches, wait for the next nor'easter to be washed away.

Fact: it is January.

A transparency over the frame: the Detective's first impression. Dissonance. A place out of place. Eliminate the setting, brush out the neighboring houses, the acid-cold pinch of the air, the perpetually overcast sky, keeping just the house framed by its orange railing, and he's not in New England but Southern California, a town with a two-word name, the second of which is always "Beach"; the home of a neon sign artist, a binary theorist, a utopian behaviorist, some Brave New World advocate, riding on the tide of tomorrow's ideas or today's vulgar and inconsequential fads—who can tell, trapped in the present tense? Not the Detective; not anymore. Possible subtitle: "The Motive." Neighbors would not like this house, or the man who built it. Difference is conflict always, if sometimes beneath the surface, and it's conflict that moves us from one frame to another.

A transparency over the frame: the eyewitness account. The time of day is dusk; the angle of vision, from within the cove; the distance, about a thousand yards. Behind the wheel of his boat, returning from a rather fruitless day of fishing, the eyewitness sees this: a figure, its limbs flailing the air midway between cliff top and water—a falling body. Shock freeze frames the image for him; then, in a series of frozen frames approximating motion, the body jerks downward toward the inevitable ocean. A pause, then the angle changes, the eyewitness drawing a straight line of vision from where the body enters the water to the promontory top. And there, leaning against the orange railing, he sees someone; too far away to identify, or even to distinguish sex or size, but a person nevertheless, and staring, he thinks, down to where the body fell. Another pause and the figure disappears as the eyewitness recovers from the initial shock and steers his boat carefully toward the walls of the cove—as close as he can come without risking the rocks. The search is futile, though, and the witness, a realist; after a half hour, he heads for home.

Fact: one does not survive a thirty-minute immersion in the January North Atlantic.

A transparency over the frame: the corrected image. Every view of a crime, the Detective has learned, is through tinted glass. The first rule: always doubt the witness; check his view before accepting the image. Note that dusk affords the poorest visibility of the day and the most deceptive. Note that dramatic and unexpected events cause selective amnesia, time distortion, astigmatic errors. And the witness himself—sober, respectable enough, no known connection to the house's occupants, but a local man, a stubborn downeaster; for him, all of reality is a frozen frame. The provincial mind, it has no doubt. "I saw what I saw," he says over and over again.

Fact: no one else has reported the "accident."

When the phone rang, the Detective was sitting in his study's easy chair, eyes closed, reading glasses at the tip of his nose, a book folded on his barreled belly. His feet were resting on a cracked leather ottoman, a concession to old age and poor circulation which failed to match the otherwise flawlessly crafted decor of the room. He made the transition from sleep to consciousness without moving his body or opening his eyes; remained that way, a disembodied mind, free of pain. Perhaps this is what death will be like, he thought, as through the study's walls, he heard his daughter's voice, an intentionally soft murmuring on the phone meant not to disturb his sleep. Strange, the Detective thought, how without understanding a word we can recognize someone's voice; how to this day he could still hear his father's cough, as distinctive as a fingerprint; how he could replay in his mind each subtle modulation in Sadie's breathing, although Sadie hadn't drawn a breath in nearly two years now. A concept occurred to the Detective then, a phrase appearing in its entirety as if by magic (he was new to this sort of thinking, this stretching the mind horizontally instead of focusing it into a bright, fine, penetrating beam)—"Identity is more than just content"—but it slipped

109

away from him like an early morning dream whose connection to reality was not obvious. And he didn't follow it. Too sleepy from his postlunch nap, diverted by his indigestion, he forgot it, and instead, thought about forgetfulness itself. Perhaps that was the true cause of senility—a loss of will, of energy, a growing inability to force the connections. Mental tenacity, he had lectured his classes in criminology, was the primary qualification of a good detective.

The Detective heard his daughter's voice rising in the next room, sensing in it excitement, trouble, incipient hysteria (for her, they were all the same), and he suddenly felt a wash of pity for her. Perhaps one of her special projects was foundering, her save-the-beach, save-the-sea-gull, save-the-old-lighthouse campaigns. The locals hated her, Charlie Wriggins had confided in him, this rich alien bitch who had lived here just five years and thought herself a native, self-crowned as Earth Mother and Defender of the Land. Sea Gull Sally, they called her. Poor famous-detective's daughter; people had always made fun of her, even when she had been a girl. She made people nervous. She had no . . . patience—that was it. And no faith. Anyone or anything she loved that wasn't within her sight was dying; she was absolutely sure of it. Her husband lying in the gutter, a mugger's knife in his back; her daughter, Nan, crushed and bleeding under the wheels of a car; her father, dead of a coronary in this very study—better check on them all to make certain they were still breathing. And now, at the onset of middle age, she had adopted the state of Maine, just as she had adopted her widowed father, certain that unless she kept a steady eye on its coastline, the shore would, in a moment's time, be swimming in oil spills and pesticide-poisoned egg shells; appeared on the beaches, just as she appeared unexpectedly in her father's study, afraid that her emotional universe would collapse without her omnipresent vigilance.

Perhaps it was his own fault. What kind of father had he been to her, involved in case after case, often away from home, and then, even when he returned, his mind preoccupied, the crime scene frame-frozen in his inner eye, the list of crisp facts clicking in his head as he searched for the solution? Preoccupied not because it was his duty, not because he was the best detective they could call on, the best they could ever call on, but because he loved it. It *was* a sin to love too much, the Detective was beginning to learn. A man was a finite vessel; emotions, energy, attention were finite gifts to be dispensed with care like the resources of his daughter's environmental plans. Love your work too much and something, someone, was bound to suffer, the vessel empty when his turn came. In the past, when he had thought about it, which wasn't often, he had believed himself to be a good husband, a good father. Now he wondered. Now he did think about it often, too often. Now the inspections were self-inspections; the framed scenes not bars and motels, but the rooms of his own home; the violations subtle, unannounced, shades of the distant past. Now there were no bleeding corpses, just memories—his wife and daughter. He had thought himself a good husband, a good father, but then he had found the letters.

The Detective opened his eyes, superimposed the visual surface of reality over his unwanted thoughts. It was as if he were glancing at a vellum scrapbook or the indexed contents of a museum exhibit, his career laid out there before him on the study's paneled walls: the medals for service, the honorary degrees and newspaper clippings, the Sherlock Holmes cap resting on the fireplace . . . all so "arranged," so dustless and dead, the room embalmed with furniture wax. And he always felt, when he first awoke here from his daily nap—eyes blinking open, body still inert—like some wax figurine, a carved prop for this historical scene: "The Famous Detective's Study,"

111

doll-house perfect. Strange, the Detective thought, how Sally hadn't changed. As a child she had played "house" with a kind of grim self-seriousness, and now, some thirty years later, the game still continued, her performance unimproved. Time was on her side, of course. Her adulthood, his old age were inevitable, the doll house a real house now, the doll a flesh-and-blood girl. But Sally wasn't satisfied with simple equality, or with just one daughter; she was intent, instead, on adopting her father, a second child to play mother to: the way she treated him since Sadie's death, the coddling, the solicitude. He had tried to resist it, but because he lacked his old tenacity, because time *was* on her side, he often gave in. Like this study, its decorations; *her* idea, done at *her* insistence: "every growing boy needs his own private room, a place to forge his identity." She always knocked now before entering the study as if afraid she would catch him masturbating.

Perhaps it's revenge, the Detective thought, some sort of emotional revenge, reversing the rage of helplessness she'd felt as a child, still felt, and inflicting . it back on her father. "Revenge"—the Detective shook his head at his choice of words. All of this psychology, this self-inspection was new to him, but the words he chose remained the same. He was still the Detective; that was the tint to his glass: his frame of reference, crime; his point of view, the criminal's.

"I will not," he heard his daughter say into the phone. A pause. She dropped to a strained whisper, but latched onto her voice, he understood her now. "He's sleeping."

The Detective straightened up, lifted his left leg by the thigh and lowered it to the floor slowly—a rush of blood, pain, life. "Sally!" he called out; closing the book on his lap, he threw it onto the roll-top desk beside him. "Sally—I'm coming!"

Sally's hurried footsteps approached the study; then (he

112

heard them in his mind just before they began), three evenly spaced knocks on his door, exclamation points for his anger, and in a moment, she was standing above him.

"Dad, you're supposed to be sleeping."

"Never you mind that. Who's on the phone for me?"

"You're supposed to take an afternoon nap every day. I didn't make that up, you know. I'm not the Bangor heart specialist who told you to start taking it easy."

"Sally . . ."

"You have to take care of yourself, Dad. You have to . . ."

"Sally," he said with emphasis. She stopped, waited, the unwilling but still obedient daughter. "It's Charlie Wriggins, isn't it?"

She pursed her lips. The Detective smiled; he lived now for these small triumphs, these feats of detection, minor victories over her insulating secrecy.

"We have to talk, Dad. You can't keep ignoring the fact that you're over seventy and have a heart condition. You have to adjust. You have to come to grips with reality."

That last phrase brought a sneer onto the Detective's face. He had heard it again and again, that almost hysterical voice pleading with her father, with her husband and daughter, with her fellow kitchen environmentalists, to come to grips with reality.

"Yes," he said, rising unsteadily, "but I suppose reality can wait till I get off the phone."

"I . . ." Sally began, then faltered; he turned around. "I hung up."

He stared at her, wordless, shocked beyond anger, waiting though for anger to come. This was new, this insulting presumption of authority, and he waited for the righteous rage of his helplessness to flood him, giving him the strength to fight

113

her back. But his rage never came; instead, he had that old sensation, a dispossession, a time suspension (if only he knew what brought on these moments, if only he could have transferred the gift to his students—the real difference between a great detective and a merely competent one): those moments when the confusion clarified, when the answer suddenly materialized, whole and inviolable. Not logic, but something like instinct which solved the mystery and yet was a mystery in itself.

"He has a case for me," the Detective said softly, half to himself.

Sally sighed; she wasn't surprised. After forty years, she was accustomed to her father's abilities, although perhaps envious of them: she had to burst through locked doors to keep informed; he merely peered through the walls.

"Look, Dad, I'm sorry, but I didn't think that you should . . ." Her apology unraveled, but he brushed it out, just as he had always brushed her and Sadie out when a case had preoccupied his mind—the absent father, the empty vessel. No, he wasn't angry with her; he was beyond emotion, disengaged and moving on another plane as Sally's voice changed, grew soft with resignation.

"He isn't home, but he did leave a number for you to call. I wrote it down on the pad by the phone." Then, one last protest, not out of hope for success, but duty-inspired. "You shouldn't, you know. You're not strong enough."

He limped quickly toward the phone. Her voice followed him there, accusatory and frightened. "He says it's murder."

The Detective dialed the number, steadying his right hand with his left by grabbing it around the wrist. He was magnanimous; he was sympathetic; he was in a forgiving mood. It had been the mentioning of murder that had frightened Sally into hanging up. Not her fault—she couldn't help seeing that knife in her husband's back, that car striking her daughter's body, that oil slick drifting inexorably toward her favorite beach. She was a worrier by nature, so he would forgive her, forgive anyone: he had a case, the first since Sadie's death.

Someone identifying himself as Officer Truax answered the phone, resisting the Detective's questions with officious inflexibility until there was an interruption from an extension.

"Hey, Sherlock, that you?"

It was Charlie Wriggin's voice, and the Detective visualized him in his mind's eye: a seventy-five-year-old, ornery and energetic ex-newspaper man who loved his profession's image and cultivated all its clichés, full of piss and vinegar and newsroom profanity. He was one of the few transplanted residents who got along with the locals (Charlie's term) because, although he was as irascible as they were, he was a reporter and not a reformer by nature; he didn't try to change their lives. The Detective waited until Officer Truax hung up.

"Where are you, Charlie?"

"The Klein place on the shore highway."

"Which one's that?"

"You've been up here two years and you don't know the Klein place? Frankly, Sherlock, you amaze me. You know, the orange erector set overlooking the cove. The one they tried to revoke the building permit on; lost in court."

"Oh yeah, the Klein place," the Detective said, but he didn't know it. A city man all his life, he had barely stepped outside since moving in with Sally, as lost in the New England countryside as a Kansas runaway in New York City. For him, Maine was a jumbled montage of sea gulls and rock and agitated ocean, a place you sent postcards from, returning home before they arrived. But now the Detective wouldn't return. Maine was his home; he would remain there until he died.

"Well, what's this all about? What happened?"

"It seems that someone—maybe Mr. Klein himself—took a walk last night." Charlie paused and the Detective sensed him savoring the drama, the headline potential of the story. "A very strange kind of walk: three feet toward Nova Scotia, and five hundred feet down into the Atlantic Ocean."

"What do you mean, 'someone'?"

"Well, the Coast Guard hasn't found the body yet. We do have a witness, but he was too far away to see who it was. And too far away to see who pushed him."

"He saw someone being pushed?"

"Not exactly. Couldn't print that, though I'd bet my next three social security checks on it."

The Detective sees desks, rows of desks, gleaming under the fluorescence of institutional lighting; he sees faces, young and attentive, propped by pencils, above open notebooks; and then, before him, a hand, his hand, chalk-smeared and gesturing, clipped with authority; his voice emerging as if from a distance, words in amber, preserved in time, to be summoned and repeated for the appropriate crimes . . .

"What's that you said?" Charlie asked him.

"I said: 'No corpse, no crime.' "

"Don't be so sure about that. Listen, Klein's missing. The only one up here is his wife and the police chief is having a hell of a time making any sense out of her. He's been here all morning and doesn't know much more than when he started. Klein was some sort of VIP scientist, and I mean the real thing—physics, the atomic bomb, a Nobel prize about ten years ago; he's practically a national asset, so we're talking about federal authorities and national press if this thing doesn't get cleared up real soon. The Chief doesn't want that, and frankly neither do I—I want this story all to myself. Now Mrs. Klein is some kind of egghead, too, so I talked the Chief

116

into letting me call you in. He's a reasonable sort for a local; knows that these intellectuals speak a language of their own. I told him you might be able to break her down, get through to her."

The Detective cleared his throat, suddenly aware of his daughter's eavesdropping presence behind him. "Can you pick me up?"

"I'll be there in fifteen minutes."

The Detective hung up, avoiding Sally as he walked back to the study. She followed him there, though, as he knew she would, and that enraged him—the predictability, the knee-jerk reflexiveness of her smothering, mothering instinct. What's the matter, he wanted to say to her sarcastically, you didn't knock this time. But he remained silent.

"You're getting involved?"

The Detective searched his desk for his pocket notebook. "I'm going to take a look around, that's all."

"You're getting involved."

The Detective turned to his daughter; searched her face for an excuse to strike out at her, for a hint of the resentment he was sure she still felt toward him. But instead, he found only a sad resignation, her eyes reflecting truths that he didn't want to see:

Fact, they said: you are seventy-two, with a heart that's older.

Fact, they said: your wife is dead and you're lost without her.

Sally shook her head and then left the room, closing the door behind her. The Detective stared after her, ashamed of himself, ashamed that her pity was so well founded. He never should have moved to Maine in the first place. After Sadie's funeral, his first few weeks of absolute solitude had frightened

117

him into accepting Sally's invitation, but now he understood that it had been a mistake. Better to have risked the loneliness, better to have risked a sudden breakdown or better yet, the blocked or burst vessel that would eventually be his end, better anything real or dramatic or painful than this slow rotting in place, this forced self-inspection, this philosophizing.

As his eyes scanned the desk, the Detective suddenly remembered the letters and he felt as if he were going to faint, heart fluttering, mouth gasping, sweat dampening his freckled forehead. He dropped into his easy chair and loosened his collar, closing his eyes. *The letters.* They were always there in the background of his mind like some vulgar jingle, popping into consciousness at the first vacant moment. And he couldn't brush them out, not the idea of them, not even their image—the white, feminine-fancy stationery, the elastic band surrounding them, the slanted curls of Sadie's script. And not the shock he had felt when, the week after the funeral, he had cleaned out her desk and found them; the suspicion. It hadn't been the sort of suspicion the Detective was accustomed to, not the professional curiosity, the teasing shadows of solutions, the pleasant, piquing mental play that directed his detection in case after case; but something more dominating and physical—nausea, paralysis, fear. And a fear that knew its object, for he had read the first two lines of the top-most letter and they had stopped him, sent him reeling. No, it hadn't been the sort of suspicion that the Detective was used to, but rather a suspicion that begged not to be confirmed: he had packed away the letters without reading another word.

A bedroom: middle class, modest in all respects, but carefully decorated, color-coordinated, its curtains and bedspread

118

a matching dark blue, its wallpaper print a floral cerulean. It is late, night, and only a small desk lamp lights the room, its corners, the edges of vision, blurred in shadows. At a writing table across from the bed, under the funneled glow of the lamp, spotlit, stage center, the woman sits, with paper and pen, a hand covering what she has written. In profile hers is a striking face, hard-planed and weathered, a middle-aged beauty, the grace of endurance, of suffering done well; but blushing now, too, as she looks to the door where the man stands, hat in his hand, shoes tracking water on the rug. Fact: it is raining outside. The room, the scene, their sudden meeting, is framed in words, her words; her eyes saying, "You should have knocked"; her refusal to avert his eyes, "I've earned my privacy." "I'm keeping a diary," she says aloud.

The man nods, accepts; he's entitling the frame, tagging it for his memory, something like—"We All Need Our Private Times." But now the Detective wanders, peering into, peering from the blurred and darkened corners, of the room, his mind; superimposing new transparencies, the tinted glass of changing realities, trying to assimilate the late-found evidence; but all grows tentative, vaporous, murky—a scene out of focus. A new subtitle floats, flirts like suspicion through the translucency of time's cataract eye: "The Lie?" But who can tell now, trapped in the present tense?

There were three sharp knocks on the study door, and they drew the Detective's attention away from the desk drawer where the letters were hidden. His heart had nearly recovered from its arrhythmic attack, but he was pale and exhausted, and the room seemed to have grown suddenly cold. He fumbled with his handkerchief, dabbing his forehead and rubbing his cheeks, futile gestures to hide the attack, and when Sally

119

entered the room with his sweater, coat, and scarf, she froze, momentarily shocked by his gray-tinged complexion. Then, recovering, she waited for the lie she knew would come.

"I'm all right," the Detective said.

Sally said nothing, slumping her shoulders, watching with a pose of passive resistance she had learned from her mother: kill yourself if you must, but I'm not going to pretend that it isn't happening.

"*I am,*" the Detective said again, but uncomfortable with the lie, he tried to escape it by hurrying on, speeding up time. He stood up quickly, reaching for his sweater; but old age demanded slow transitions, from sleep into consciousness, from sitting into standing, was a slow transition itself from life into death. His left leg, gravity-pumped, swelled with blood, ached until he thought he would cry out from it, then buckled at the knee and he began to fall. He threw out his hand to catch the desk and brace himself, but Sally's arms, younger, quicker, were there first, gathering him around the chest and pulling him toward her. He hung there, dead weight, a drowned body, his heart racing helplessly again, waiting for the slow transition out of pain.

For a moment, the Detective gave in to it; more than physically he surrendered his resistance and clung to his daughter. It occurred to him then to ask her. It occurred to him then that she might know, and that even if she didn't, just to share the burden, to transfer it, letting her ask the questions he couldn't ask, letting her read the lines he couldn't read—letting her be the detective—would be a relief. But what was he to ask her, how was he to phrase it? "Did your mother, did your mother always love me? Was she always, did she ever . . . ?" Words faded; pain faded, pumped away by a steadier heart, replaced by anger, self-disgust. That he should

120

have to ask Sally in order to know; that she should know and not he; that she should have been closer to Sadie than he . . . The Detective placed his hand on the desk and pushed himself away from her.

"Let go of me," he said.

Sally dropped her arms, slowly at first, ready to support him again if he weren't strong enough to stand on his own. She refused to look at his face—for his sake, his pride, the shame she knew he felt at his dependence on her; and, too, for her own sake, to avoid the hate she knew she'd find in his eyes. And the Detective hated her even more for that further kindness—her refusal to rub it in. Fact: their roles *had* reversed. That she believed that and still tried at times like these to pretend she didn't only emphasized its truth all the more to him. He was close to Sally now, closer than he had ever been before, but he had never loved her less. Inequality bred dependence, bred closeness, bred hate and resentment. That she should know and not he . . . no, he wouldn't, he couldn't ask. The Detective reached for his sweater and, turning his back to his daughter, buttoned it slowly, taking refuge in the independence of a simple task.

A car horn honked from the driveway. The Detective hurriedly threw on his coat and scarf, and then, avoiding Sally's eyes by looking toward the floor, he left the room, hoping to avert another confrontation. But by the time he reached the front door, he was acutely conscious of an obligation to reassure her, aware that she would worry as soon as he left her sight. He paused there in the doorway and turned to face her; there were tears in her eyes, tears he had caused.

"Don't go, Dad," she said. "You know you're not up to it."

Sally reached out tentatively, touching his plaid scarf, a gesture so pathetic that the Detective wanted to slap her hand

121

away and to slap away with it all the closeness and dependence and guilt he felt. But his revulsion passed quickly, and instead, he felt sorry for her, bound to her all the more. Sea Gull Sally, the habitual worrier—what had he done to her that she had so little faith? and what had happened to him that he was becoming so like her? The Detective kissed his daughter on the cheek, squeezed her hand reassuringly.

"I'll be all right," he said.

But as he walked down the steps toward Charlie Wriggins's car, he knew that he wasn't all right. All the hope that Charlie's phone call had aroused in him was suddenly gone, Sally's oppressive despair in its place: . . . those strange thoughts which afflicted him now, those concepts that stretched beyond comprehension, so unlike the measured facts of detection—what was he to do with them? what did they mean? Despair was the province of a philosopher, not a detective. To a man without hope, the world appeared hopeless; a man with hope, foolish—but was it actually so? The first rule: always doubt the witness. The Detective no longer trusted his own judgments; everything had become tentative, vaporous, murky. Come to grips with reality, his daughter had told him, but which reality, whose reality? Sally's? Charlie's? His own?

And even as he drove to the Klein house, captive audience to Charlie Wriggins's manic enthusiasm, despair wouldn't leave the Detective. He turned in the seat, pretending to listen, his attention though directed inward; and staring through the windshield into the formless slate of the sky, he thought: "Even murder can't excite me anymore." It was as if he were dead or anesthetized. But then another realization— unsolicited, unwanted—followed: it was as if he were on another case, preoccupied and withdrawn, seeking the solution, and nothing, not even murder, could divert his attention from it. Yes, he was on another case, although he fought it, forcing it from consciousness whenever he could, although he wished more than anything else that the case would disappear. And as they drove toward the ocean, toward the Klein house, toward the scene of the crime, the Detective projected onto that blank and depthless sky, as though it were the blackboard of his old classroom or a clean page in his pocket notebook, the skeletal clues of the other crime, the one that would not leave him. And he saw written there the words of his own mind; recorded, preserved in time, as objective and relentless as the aching in his thighs. Fact, he saw there, fact: I've never found her diary.

2

The Detective sat in what he assumed to be the Kleins' living room, although it was like no living room he had ever seen: tubular, stainless steel chairs twisted into geometric shapes, with glittering, curved lucite backs as smooth as polished marble; bright orange wall-to-wall carpeting as luxuriant as a field of ripening wheat, the pile hiding the furniture's feet so that the chairs seemed rooted there, sprung flowers of extraterrestrial origin, the science fiction garden of a World's Fair exhibit; three of its walls a flat and spotless white, and bare except for a series of evenly spaced paintings which in an ordered progression grew from the size of a postage stamp on the first wall to a three-foot square on the third. The paintings were formless swatches and splashes of color, reds and oranges, and they reminded the Detective of his own mind, an eruption of thoughts, boiling and swirling like lava, seeking the bottom ground, the cooling ocean, inert and settled form. A stainless steel mobile hung from the center of the ceiling; in constant chaotic motion, its individual parts, shiny metallic propellers, spun against each other—a separate mechanical universe with its own complex of rules and conflicts whose unfolding gave the Detective a headache.

But more disconcerting to him, the strangest aspect of all, was the room's shape. A triangle whose top had been sliced off, its walls joined at oblique angles, each chair situated so that it had at least a three-quarter frontal view of the triangle's wide base, the fourth wall, that wall made of a single sheet of glass—not a picture window, but a full wall of glass. And stretching behind it, as if some vacationer's snapshot, a mammoth color slide flashed upon the wall, were the cliff, the promontory rock, the cove, the orange metal walkway leading to them all, and beyond, as far as the eye could see, the ocean. The scene of the crime, frozen there before their eyes. Only the gulls and terns seemed alive, arching, swooping, diving into the funneled depths of the cove, then rising effortlessly on invisible thrusts of wind, arrogant and free. Toy-sized in the distance, a Coast Guard cutter rocked in the cove's mouth, searching for the body.

"Let's go through it one more time, all right, Mrs. Klein?"

The police chief spoke slowly; he was exhausted and on the edge of exasperation, yet still polite. The Detective tried to brush out the others from his sight—Charlie Wriggins, Officer Truax, the eyewitness called Dexter—and concentrated on the Chief and Mrs. Klein. This review was for his sake, he knew, and he was conscious of intruding into another man's case, a feeling difficult to erase with Officer Truax glaring at him from the corner.

"All right," the police chief said again, the Detective noting his heavy-lidded and expressionless face, "let's start from the top then. Last night, at about five o'clock, Dexter here, coming back into dock, saw a body fall into the cove. He also saw someone else standing at the top of the cliff, near to the point from where—he assumed—the body must have fallen." The Chief paused, breathed deeply as if the sentence had been too complex and mentally exhausting for him. "Unfortunately, though, due to the distance and poor light, he couldn't recognize either of the two people. Have I got that right, Dexter?"

Dexter, rail-thin, stood in the center of the room, his feet buried in the rug pile like a pier post at low tide. His hair was a salt-bleached gray, his face a parched red; his eyes, tiny and black, clung above his cheeks like barnacle shells. A crucifix of defiance, he stared straight ahead as he spoke.

"I saw what I saw," he said.

"All right. So what we have, then, are two nameless people, one presumably dead and one who presumably saw him die but for some unknown reason failed to report it to the Coast Guard or the police. Now the logical thing to do would be to try to identify who those two people were, starting with the presumed deceased. Dexter couldn't find the body last night and, as of this moment anyway, the Coast Guard hasn't had any luck either. So, what we're left with, then, is the process of elimination. Now Officer Truax and myself know all the full-time residents of this area and it didn't take long to ascertain that none were missing. That left the part-time residents such as Mr. and Mrs. Klein. Now Officer Truax and myself keep a list of phone numbers where those part-time residents can be reached in case of theft or damage to their property up here. So we called those numbers, last night and all this morning, and as of right now, the only person not accounted for is Mr. Klein. Am I right on that, Officer Truax?"

A clipped nod. "Right."

"All right. So what we have is this. Either the person who fell last night from the cliff into the cove was Mr. Klein or it was someone who had no business being up here. Now this *is* Mr. Klein's property; he *does* have business being up here."

The Chief inhaled laboriously. He leaned forward in his stainless steel chair, focusing on Mrs. Klein, and the Detective sensed in him then something of the law itself—plodding, implacable, relentlessly inhumanly patient.

"Mrs. Klein," he said, "where is your husband?"

Mrs. Klein sat in one of the room's obliquely angled corners beside the wall of glass, dwarfed by the dimensions of the coastal setting. And for a moment, the Detective's mind seemed to expand, embracing that contrast between the size of the woman and the immensity of the world she had been born into; it seemed to stretch, groping toward some concept bigger than the person and the scene inspiring it, a concept tagged with words like "folly," "awe," "futility." But now no longer alone in his study, no longer merely biding time, the Detective resisted the philosophizing which had begun to dominate his mental life, those drifting, irrational sequences he secretly found compelling but feared were a sign of encroaching senility and death. Instead, he shrunk the borders of his vision, focusing not on what this woman meant, but on who she was—this could-be widow, this suspect.

He guessed that she was in her fifties, her hair cropped short and fully gray, her clothing—dark stockings, short plaid skirt, a fisherman's turtleneck sweater—campus style. Her eyes were white-rimmed and protuberant, hyperthyroidal; they cast about the room in an endless, jittery search of the floor as if she had lost her wedding ring there. Perhaps she had. The Detective saw no ring on either hand, but found little significance in that fact. Traditions, the old symbols, meant nothing anymore, especially to the sort of people who built stainless steel and glass living rooms. Sadie, the Detective remembered, immediately trying to squelch the memory, had never removed her wedding ring, that thin gold band melding with her skin; she'd been buried with it on. And he sees her now, framed in mahogany, a plush silken background, the scent of flowers so overwhelmingly sweet that he feels he may vomit from it, her cheeks so pale that the mortician's rouge can't cover their lifelessness—as he bends, now and forever slowly bending, and removing his ring, drops it on her chest. The Detective stared at his left hand; the ring finger, freckled, swollen, showed no sign of the band he had worn there for nearly fifty years. No, the old symbols meant nothing anymore—maybe they never had—but he'd ask Mrs. Klein about it later anyway. "A case," he hears himself lecture over and over, words in amber, "is solved with details."

"Mrs. Klein," the Chief repeated after receiving no answer. "*Where* is your husband?"

"I, I don't know. I just don't know." She frowned, surprised at herself, as if she were perplexed by her own lack of knowledge.

"Were you here at the house last night?"

"Yes. Here."

"Well, was your husband with you then?"

Mrs. Klein said nothing; refused even to lift her head, her eyes still involved in their frantic searching, like . . . like REMs, the Detective suddenly thought, rapid eye movements that signified dreaming during sleep, as if although awake, she were still living in last night's dream.

"Mrs. Klein," the police chief said. He sighed. "Mrs. Klein, now that's a simple question. Your husband—was he or was he not with you last night?"

"I . . . I don't know. He might have been. It seems to me

127

that, that . . ." She picked at short, silver strands of hair that covered her ear; her voice dropped: "He might have been."

There was an uneasy pause. Then, Dexter, the eyewitness, his gaze directed at no one in particular, broke in, reminding them that he considered the entire procedure an attack on his honor.

"I saw what I saw," he said again.

Mrs. Klein looked up quickly. "I don't doubt that," she said. "I don't doubt that at all. You saw what you saw; see what you see; will see what you will see—when you see it. I don't doubt that at all."

She stared at Dexter for a moment, her eyes finally focused, steady, but when he refused to acknowledge her, she panicked, glancing quickly around the room for confirmation. Out of the corner of his eye, the Detective noticed Charlie Wriggins gesturing to him, an I-told-you-so expression on his face.

"Yes," the Chief said at last. "Well." He stood up. "Why don't you freshen yourself up a bit, Mrs. Klein? I realize all of this has been quite a trial for you."

Without giving her a chance to respond, the Chief crossed the room and gently lifted her by the elbow from her seat. He led her to the door, the others watching her unsteady, bewildered, sleepwalk shuffle—all but the Detective who, taking advantage of that short moment of privacy, gradually straightened his left leg. (He mustn't let them see how lame he was.) By the time the Chief had returned to the living room, the Detective was standing, his secret concealed, the pain in his leg a dull and bearable ache, no longer visible on his face. Charlie Wriggins, notebook in hand, and Officer Truax had risen too, and the four of them huddled there in the center of the room beneath the twisting stainless steel propellers of the mobile. Only Dexter stood apart.

"Well," the Chief said, his eyes neutral, conceding nothing, "what do you think?"

"Is she always like that?" the Detective asked.

"No one up here seems to know. Her husband did most of the errands around town. They didn't spend much time up here anyway—their second home. Mainly in the summer."

"It could be from shock," the Detective said. "But the question is, shock from what? From being informed that her husband might be dead? From having seen him die? From having killed him?—You don't have any physical evidence that Mr. Klein was up here last night?"

The Chief shook his head. "That's the strange thing. No food in the cabinets; no garbage. For Christsake, we even had to turn the water on. It's just as if the house had been closed up for the winter, as if neither of them had been here in months. There's not even a car in the garage. Now how the hell did she get up here, I keep asking myself. I already checked the one taxi in the area—no fares to the Klein house since September, the driver says. One more thing for whatever it's worth. These drapes were open when we came in; it was the only sign that the house was occupied—besides Mrs. Klein herself, that is."

"There's men's clothing in the closets," Officer Truax said.

The Chief shook his head. "Means nothing. They're all summer clothes. When you're as rich as the Kleins, you don't bother carrying wardrobes around with you. You just keep full closets in all your houses."

The Detective thought a moment and then said, "What's his size?"

Officer Truax, stung by the Chief's dismissal, laughed sarcastically. "What, you want his hand-me-downs?"

"Truax," the Chief said. He sighed, then looked up to the ceiling, seemed to study the intricate motions of the mobile.

How patient he is, the Detective thought, how controlled. "Truax, he's talking about the man, not his clothes." The Chief turned to the Detective. "He was a big one all right, bigger than you. But that doesn't eliminate Mrs. Klein as a suspect; she still could have pushed him, tiny as she is. Just take a look at that walkway out there; it was built with the view, not safety, in mind."

The three of them, all but Dexter, followed the Chief's pointed hand and stared through the glass wall to the cove. The Coast Guard cutter was half blocked from view by the promontory rock; the sky, as gray as the cutter's hull, was so overcast that the time of day was indiscernible.

"The body," the Dectective said, "is there much chance of recovery?"

The Chief shook his head. "No, and that means, unfortunately, that even if she did do it . . . ."

The Detective nodded, completing the thought for him. "No corpse, no crime," he said.

Charlie Wriggins broke in: "But you've got a witness."

The Chief glanced at Dexter. "Who witnessed a falling body, not someone pushing that body. We'd never even make it to court on his testimony. Not without a confession. Well, any suggestions?"

The Detective hesitated: the Chief's eyes still veiled his mood, his motives, but there was no time left for stalling. Tact, the Detective lectured himself, be tactful, courteous; no swaggering, no arrogance.

"It does occur to me that a woman in Mrs.Klein's condition . . . well, that she might be frightened, confused by so many people."

He paused. The Chief stared at him—a cop's stare, suspicious, penetrating. "You want to speak to her alone?"

130

"It might be helpful. Someone out of uniform. Give her a chance to relax; a simple conversation instead of an interrogation."

The Chief said nothing, and the Detective watched him as he made up his mind, sympathizing with him, knowing from experience the painful conflict he was going through: duty versus personal pride. To have invited the Detective in as a consultant was excusable, but to leave him alone with the major suspect was to concede his own failure and to permit the possibility of the crime being solved without his own participation.

The Chief sighed. "All right. It can't hurt. I'll leave Truax outside in the patrol car to guard the place and relay any messages. Charlie here will give Dexter and me a ride back to town. It's what, three o'clock now? I'll give you till six or so unless something comes up in the meantime."

Charlie broke in to protest his exclusion from the questioning. The Chief listened to him briefly, a slight ironic smile on his face, the first sign of emotion he had displayed since the Detective's arrival.

"Right, Charlie," he said. "Just what we need to calm her down—a reporter recording every word out of her mouth. No, you go with the rest of us. And besides, we need the ride, don't we, Dexter?"

Dexter said nothing. A moment later, Mrs. Klein reentered the room, freezing the conversation in its silence. She stopped in front of the glass wall and stared out to the cove.

"I better let her know what's going on," the Chief said softly. "The rest of you get going. I'll be out in a minute."

Dexter, Truax, and Charlie Wriggins grabbed their coats and silently left the house. The Detective stood to the side and watched the Chief, a man of formidable bulk and pres-

131

ence in his dark blue uniform, as with hat in hand he lowered himself to Mrs. Klein's level and explained to her gently that he would return in a few hours. The Detective admired the Chief then, admired his patience and gentleness, the character it had taken to let the case out of his personal control; and he reexperienced through his admiration the sense of common mission which had always enhanced his love of detection, felt again that sense of higher duty, of belonging to a whole, a whole which, extending beyond the individual self, was defined by a devotion to one shared goal: solving the crime. The good ones always knew it. The prizes and medals, the media attention, none of that mattered; the one-man-against-the-multitude-of-evil image, the Sherlock Holmes syndrome, was the province of fictional romance, not reality. That the Detective understood and accepted this was both the source of his sincere humility and, to a degree, the secret of his professional success. He knew that individuals in and of themselves could rarely solve a case. It was the backing of a team, the consolidated effort, the combined and therefore relentless pressure of society's law that crushed the sordid and private mystery of a crime. The good detective merely directed the mass, discovered the pressure point where the weight of the law, once applied, would be irresistible.

The Chief had finished with Mrs. Klein. He walked with the Detective to the front door where he stopped, turned, and, after a pause, accepted the Detective's hand, shaking it with quick, vigorous jerks. A professional exchange; not friendship but respect—teammates.

"Chief," the Detective said, finally dropping his hand. "I've been meaning to ask you about Dexter."

"Oh, yes, Dexter. Well, he's reliable, if that's what you mean. You'll have to take my word on that for now, and you'll have to know the people around here a little better to understand it. They may not make much of a living or break any records for friendliness, but they do make great witnesses. Oh yeah, I believe him. It happened, all right . . ."

The police chief paused, placed his hat on his head and, staring past the Detective to Mrs. Klein and her glass-wall view of the promontory point, said:

". . . whatever 'it' is."

The Detective sat in the living room and attempted without success to adapt his sagging, aging body to the inflexible curves of his steel and lucite chair. Mrs. Klein, her back to him, stood ten feet away, silently staring through the glass wall toward the cove, her arms clasped from cold or fear—a fisherman's wife keeping an uneasy vigil, waiting for her husband's return from the sea.

"Are you feeling any better?" the Detective said. "I could make some coffee if you'd like."

"We have no coffee." She spoke without turning her head, an emotionless fact, a truism. "We don't believe in coffee."

"I'm afraid I don't understand."

"We don't believe in artificial stimulation."

"Oh—bad for the heart, I suppose. Actually, I shouldn't have any myself; just decaffeinated."

"Bad for the mind."

"What's that?"

"We believe it's bad for the mind. We believe artificial stimulation is unnecessary, excessive. We believe the brain is biochemically sufficient without the addition of artificial stimulants."

"Oh." The Detective frowned, as puzzled by the delivery as by the words themselves. There was something about her insistence on the plural, there was something about her em-

133

phasis of that "we" that made him wonder if she were being bitter or ironic; but without seeing her face, he couldn't be sure.

"Yes, well, when you get to be my age you begin to wonder. Nothing in your body seems sufficient by itself."

"You don't have to reach your age . . ." Mrs. Klein said; she paused and then added, as if she only grudgingly accepted a responsibility to be more than cryptic, ". . . to wonder."

"I understand," the Detective said, although he wasn't certain that he did. "It's the waiting. It's the not knowing. Don't worry—something should turn up soon; something definite."

Mrs. Klein faced him for the first time; she turned, tilting her head, her arms clasped beneath her breasts. Her protuberant eyes were steady now, attentive and yet distracting still, their transformation from boredom to interest too sudden and complete.

"Is that what you think—that it's the not knowing?" She walked to a chair and sat down in it. "But then, you're a detective, aren't you?"

"Yes."

"And it's your job—to know, I mean; to come up with something definite."

"In a manner of speaking."

"My husband's a detective in a manner of speaking."

"Yes, I was told that he was a scientist." The Detective flinched at his use of the past tense, but Mrs. Klein didn't appear to notice it. "A physicist, they said."

"Yes, a physicist, but a detective nevertheless, a detective in a manner of speaking. Not knowing bothers him too; coming up with something definite is his job too. Matter in motion, that's his field, pieces of matter so small that they can never be seen by the human eye. He worked on the atomic bomb."

134

"Yes, I believe someone mentioned that."

"Aren't you going to ask if we feel guilty about it—the atomic bomb, I mean?"

"I don't think . . ."

"We don't believe in guilt. Oh, it exists, but we don't believe in its importance other than as a corrective adjustment for future behavior. We believe guilt is a feedback mechanism."

The Detective shifted in his chair. There was no doubt in his mind now; he saw bitterness in her face, heard sarcasm in her words—the overemphasis on the "we," the mock blank expression—and instinctively he began to think of motive. Sarcasm negated meaning: "We don't believe in guilt" enunciated that way meant that she *did* believe in guilt, that she felt guilty. Or at least that she disliked her husband's lack of guilt. But ideas do not motives make, the Detective told himself. Wives do not kill their husbands because they worked on the atomic bomb; it was always more petty, irrational, personal. Murder was a personal act, the Detective had come to learn, though often rationalized by grander notions. Perhaps Mrs. Klein had convinced herself otherwise; but if she had killed Mr. Klein, the true motive would lie in the slough of their everyday lives, the balance of power between husband and wife, the subtle shades of emotional betrayal, the knife-glances and abused intimacies, the resenting of someone who knew her too well.

"And you," Mrs. Klein said, her eyes growing wider, circular and white-rimmed, "do you believe in guilt?"

A frame, blurred frame, discolored from age (what day, what year, which moment, or is it many moments recomposed into one?); in it a chair, shapeless and unclear (which chair? whose chair? try to remember, to focus the picture but all that appears is *the chair*, an abstraction, an idea); Sadie in the chair, Sadie not abstract, Sadie now and forever a face in a moment, a profile turning toward him, pride smoldering in silence . . . all her accusing glances merged into one: "The Motive?" "The Motives?"

"But of course," she said, "you're the detective, the criminal investigator, and the detective must believe in the assignment of guilt—first degree and second degree, felony and misdemeanor. That's your job, after all."

"No, that's not my job." The Detective sat up, a sore point struck, an argument he had fought time and time again. "Guilt is subjective; it's assigned by the judge, by the jury. I, I just . . ."

"You detect."

"Yes, I detect. I tell them what happened."

"The objective truth."

"The objective truth; as close as I can come to it."

"Your subjective view of the objective truth."

The Detective watched Mrs. Klein, uncertain of her intent, unable to enter a rhythm of conversation because he didn't know what to anticipate next. She sat five feet from him, legs and arms crossed, a knot of intensity, her shorn head stretched forward in expectation of an answer from him—sincere, too sincere; serious, too serious; and above all, too logical, the supralogic of the insane. Her eyes were drawn into a stare too focused to sustain, the Detective waiting uneasily for them to jerk into their jittery searching again. Beyond all this, though, beyond the facts before his eyes, her physical presence, was the suspicion that she was acting, this entire conversation a contemptuous deception, the murderess's self-defense. But a suspicion based on what—what besides the paranoia he had absorbed from Sally lately? The Detective wasn't sure, and sitting within the Klein living room, that oddly antiseptic opening to the stark Maine coast, he felt himself trapped in some visual conundrum, the impossible metaphor of his own confusion, poised at a fulcrum where paired opposites met—time and timelessness, nature and artifice, pity and suspiciousness, all coming full circle and fusing at a border as paradoxical as glass.

"No answer for me, Descartes?" Mrs. Klein said. "Too confused to answer?—It's the not knowing, isn't it? It's the not knowing that upsets you so. Don't worry, Descartes; something should turn up soon. Something definite."

Sarcastic and yet pitying, contemptuous and yet compassionate—the Detective couldn't be sure. Although they were not at all alike physically, in some illogical way that he couldn't quite conceptualize, this strange woman, this murder suspect, reminded him of his wife; aroused in him a similar complex of conflicting emotions, a frustrating urge both to accuse and embrace, to punish and console. Yes, that was it; Mrs. Klein was right, the Detective suddenly understood; it *was* the not knowing that bothered him so, the lack of certainty that paralyzed him with second thoughts and indecision. If he knew, if only he knew which were true: grieving widow or deceiving murderess; loving, loyal wife or . . . The Detective thought of Sally; missed her. She would be in the kitchen now, at the table or at the stove, on the phone, keeping informed while making supper, a vigilant ear for incipient trouble; and he could almost hear spoons striking pots, the familiar tattoo of her knife against the cutting board, the way those sounds eased into consciousness as he lay half-asleep in his shuttered study. That was his reality now; not crime or detection, not the intimate dance of interrogation, but the muffled preparation of the bourgeois dinner—soft, safe, distant.

"I say that to Andy," Mrs. Klein said. "I've said it for years now. It's a joke, an in-joke. You know, the sort of silly thing that couples share?"

The Detective nodded. He knew; he knows: the wine mispronounced on their first wedding anniversary is mispronounced on the second, and on the third, and on the tenth, is forever mispronounced, and no one else may mispronounce it, an exclusive right of Sadie's and his, giving shape to their marriage, to their special, secret life together—now and forever.

"Whenever he's stumped, whenever he's reached a dead end in his work, whenever those tiny pieces of matter in motion have confused him so much that he begins to despair of ever finding out the truth about them, I say to him, 'Don't worry, Descartes, something will turn up.' It's an in-joke now, one of those little rituals that make up a marriage, one of those little boosts that sustain our momentum. It keeps him going, he says. I'm his inspiration, he says. His accomplice."

"His accomplice?"

Mrs. Klein ignored his question. "Should I do that for you—be your inspiration, help you to discover something definite? Should I become your accomplice?"

"About your husband," the Detective said, trying to initiate the interrogation.

"Yes, about my husband. Do you think he's dead?"

The Detective blinked, his hands fumbling with his pocket notebook; stunned, he stared at her for a moment. The question had been normal, but the manner of its asking, incredible—intellectual curiosity, as if she were working on some academic problem.

"I'm . . . well, I'm skeptical, let's put it that way. What about you?"

138

"Yes," Mrs. Klein said, "that makes sense. You're skeptical—the definite knower, the objective truth-seeker, the detective. Andy, who is a detective in a manner of speaking, has always promoted skepticism. We believe in it."

"Yes, Mrs. Klein, but your husband, right now: do you think that he's dead or alive?"

Mrs. Klein looked away from him, her sarcasm suddenly failing her, her eyes gone manic again, caught up in their waking dream, searching, searching. Her loss of control frightened the Detective, but excited him too, his blood-instinct aroused by her sudden vulnerability, by the appearance of a pressure point that he could use.

"At this moment, Mrs. Klein, at this exact moment, is your husband dead or alive?"

The Detective tried to lean forward in his chair, to press home the question with his physical presence, his body resisting with its inertial pain, Mrs. Klein avoiding his insistent stare.

"Why must you know? Why do you have to keep on the trail? What if I told you that whatever happened, it was for the best—couldn't you just leave it at that?"

She knew; she did know. "Dead or alive, Mrs. Klein?"

Mrs. Klein hid her face in her hands. "I", she began, "I believe . . ." She paused, measuring her breaths, gaining control by degrees. She dropped her hands, lifting her face to meet his stare; yes, she nodded to herself, yes. Her eyes had begun to steady themselves.

"We believe he's alive."

She had slipped away from him; he had allowed her to slip away, into her sarcasm or her pretense of sarcasm, out of her vulnerability, the pressure point so visible just a moment before suddenly gone. The Detective was tired, felt a tepid disgust for his own inadequacy. Fact: he was losing his touch. He no longer had the mental tenacity, the will required to force the connections—he didn't really want to. Something was missing, a subtraction of old age, some basic drive dried up, that insatiable desire for solution. But he must try; if only to keep his life coherent, if only out of allegiance to his old self-image, he must try to finish it. And so he stalled, staring at the blank pages of his notebook, twisting his feet in the orange carpet, as he tried to organize his thoughts.

"Mrs. Klein, when did you arrive here? Exactly how long have you been up here?"

"Always."

"You've always been up here—with no food or water."

"In a manner of speaking."

"I'm not interested in manners of speaking. I'm interested in facts, times of arrival and departure, confirmed and witnessed events; facts concerning your husband's disappearance."

"I don't doubt that," she said. "I don't doubt that at all. It makes perfect sense that you should. You're the detective and the detective believes in facts; the detective sees what he sees."

"Well, then, perhaps you'd like to give me some facts to believe in. For example, was your husband here at the house last night?"

"Yes."

"He was here?"

"He's always here."

"He's not here now, Mrs. Klein; that's a fact I believe in."

"You see what you see when you see it." She tilted her head, considered him. "You *do* think he's dead, don't you? That's your subjective view of the objective truth."

Curiosity again; the wrong mood at the wrong time—

140

always. The Detective watched her helplessly and felt that she was toying with him, that she had become the interrogator and he the suspect.

"Perhaps," he said.

"And perhaps you believe that I killed him. But then, you can't be sure about that, can you? You must be skeptical, mustn't you?"

The Detective sighed—no, he hadn't the endurance any longer; the mockery, the convolutions of their conversation exhausted and confused him, made him impatient. His bad leg, stationary since the others had left, its already poor circulation pinched by the hard edge of his lucite chair, had gone numb, radiating needles of pain. He winced from it, cried out from its suddenness and surprise, reaching down with both hands and squeezing his thigh just above the knee. Mrs. Klein leaped from her chair in a panic of concern and hovered over him, a confusing form on the periphery of his attention, for he could only focus on the pain, the pain and the fear that his heart, erratically racing, would burst or simply stop, too exhausted to go on. Slowly, though, as the pain ebbed, as his heart regained a steadier rhythm, the Detective became aware of her presence above him: her fingers, weightless spots of cold, touched his brow in a healer's gesture, a priest's blessing; her voice lapped over him, gentle waves of some deep, embracing calm.

"Don't worry, Descartes," she said over and over again. "Something will turn up. Don't worry, Descartes, your accomplice is here."

The Detective straightened up, releasing his thigh, drawing his forehead away from her icy touch while avoiding her eyes. His frailty fully revealed now, he was ashamed and afraid, feeling that their relationship had changed, sensing that a

141

kind of equality had been reached, a parity of pain: widow and widower, teammates in suffering, caught up in this mystery by the fact of their survival; lost together. And for the first time, he believed her without qualification; accepted the sincerity of her offer without understanding its meaning.

"I'll help you," she said. "I'll be your accomplice."

There was a pause; she waited there silently above him— for confirmation, he knew, for a commitment on his part, some visible sign of his willing participation. The Detective waited, too; and then, without understanding why, he felt himself nod.

"All right," Mrs. Klein said, her sarcasm instantly return- ing, mockery of the Chief's methodical style, "let's start from the top." She turned and began pacing. "Last night at about five o'clock, a local fisherman named Dexter saw what he saw. And what he saw was a body falling from the promontory point into the cove. Now who could this body be, we ask ourselves? The property from which said body fell belonged to a Mr. and Mrs. Andrew Klein, Nobel prize-winning physicist and obscure medieval historian respectively, and a thorough check has revealed that Mr. Klein, despite his Nobel prize, is missing. Tentative conclusion: Mr. Klein is what the local fisherman named Dexter saw when he saw what he saw. Am I right so far?"

The Detective nodded.

"So the question is, how do we proceed from here? Now what would Andy do, I ask myself? How would Andy, who has been a detective in a manner of speaking all his life, approach the problem of the disappearance of one Andrew Klein?"

"Possibilities," the Detective said. "List all the possibilities and then analyze them, eliminating the unlikely ones."

"That's it, that's what Andy would do: proceed scientifically. We believe in the scientific method. The possibilities . . ."

"Accident, murder, suicide, fake death," the Detective interrupted, seeing his hand trace the letters on a smudged slate blackboard.

Mrs. Klein sat down abruptly, crossed her legs, folded her arms, her head craned forward—wound energy about to explode. "But surely you've forgotten one."

The Detective shook his head. "I don't think . . ."

"Sacrifice, what about a sacrifice?"

"I don't understand."

"A human sacrifice. An appeasement to the gods, to nature. Diving into the volcano's mouth in order to prevent the catastrophe. A symbolic act. A ritual of penance. An atonement."

"An atonement for what?"

"For going where he was forbidden to go; for knowing what he was forbidden to know; for killing what he cared about most without even being aware of it. For hubris. A man who has violated the secrets of those tiny pieces of matter in motion, a man who has worked on the atomic bomb, has a great deal to atone for, wouldn't you say?"

The Detective didn't reply, endured her sarcasm as it reached a peak of purity and then surpassed it, becoming anger. Her voice shook, dropped to a husky, wavering accusation.

"But no, no, you're the detective, aren't you? You're one of us and we don't believe in guilt, do we? It's subjective; we leave atonement for the judges and juries to decide. All we care about is what happened, something definite, the objective truth. We see what we see when we see it, and nothing more, don't we?"

"No, I don't think that's true," the Detective said. "We wouldn't know very much if it were—only ourselves, only our own lives. We can deduce, we can listen to others, we can make educated guesses. We can from our past experience suggest possibilities and then analyze them." The Detective paused, tempted, excited by the ideas, drawn once again into the impulse to philosophize; but he resisted it, this desire to generalize, to expand and connect, and instead began to dissect.

"For example, the fake death possibility. Its motive is almost always an escape: from debt, from an unhappy marriage, from punishment for a crime already committed; sometimes it's accompanied by a large life insurance policy, and the benefactor is his accomplice. But does that scenario fit the facts? Does it fit the particular features of this particular case? One advantage to this possibility: it does explain the second person, the one who the eyewitness saw at the railing. If a dummy had been thrown off the promontory point, that other person could have been Mr. Klein himself. And that, in turn, would explain the absence of a car here—Mr. Klein drove away in it after faking his own death. But then we turn to the liabilities. In order to fake a death, in order to convince police officials and insurance investigators, he would need a witness, someone he had fooled into thinking that he had actually died. True, we do have Dexter, but Dexter was in a boat a thousand yards away or more, in poor light. There's no way Mr. Klein could have assumed that Dexter would even be looking in the right direction at the right moment. Not unless Dexter is his accomplice, which, on the surface at least, would seem highly unlikely."

The Detective felt himself expanding, a lifetime of intelligent work, of specialized thinking, unfolding from him ef-

144

fortlessly. And he began to feel as well that controlled joy of mastery, that self-consciousness of one's own competence in the midst of the action itself, which had propelled him into case after case and had kept him preoccupied, despite the hours, the fatigue—despite his wife and child.

"So what we have, then, is a possibility, but an unlikely one. So we push that to the side for a moment. We don't eliminate it. We still check on insurance policies and personal debts; we still make sure that Dexter hasn't come into a sudden fortune. But for the moment, we push it to the side and look for a more probable solution. Are you with me so far?"

"Yes," Mrs. Klein said, her voice suddenly gone flat again. "Probability. We proceed according to probability; that makes perfect sense."

"Okay. We have three other possibilities then: accident, suicide, murder. But if we look at the facts—the facts, Mrs. Klein, the few pieces of information available to us—if we consider them, letting our minds stretch to meet their implications, one specific fact stands out from all the others; seems to tell us more, to hint at a solution. And do you know which fact that is, Mrs. Klein?"

Mrs. Klein didn't look at him, seemed to have lost her interest in the case. "The other person," she said in a monotone, "the one at the railing."

"That's right, Mrs. Klein. Fact: the person seen at the railing did not report the fall. Now if it had been an accident or suicide, why wouldn't the person have called the Coast Guard or the police or run to a neighbor's house? There are possibilities, of course, but are they likely ones, are they probable? Do you see what I mean, Mrs. Klein?'

"So you think it's murder; that's your subjective view of the objective truth."

145

No sarcasm this time, but no real interest either—just a tepid curiosity. The Detective was disappointed; yes, it was his tentative view of the facts that they seemed to point to murder, but he realized suddenly that the conclusion itself wasn't what mattered to him. Instead, he had wanted to prove the philosophical point; had wanted to demonstrate that we can know more than what we see, extending ourselves beyond the moment of our experience. No, more than that, he had wanted to defend a state of mind, a way of thinking, his profession, his life in fact; had wanted her to withdraw the accusing glances and sarcasm, and then, acceptance won, to stand over her, victorious in his detective's competence— vindicated. And when he realized this, when he realized that he cared more about Mrs. Klein's opinion of himself than he cared about the case, more about his own guilt or innocence than hers, all of his professional enthusiasm seemed nothing more than a plea for . . . for what—affirmation? An old man begging someone he barely knew, a murder suspect, to tell him that his life had been worthwhile?

Years ago, before her death, only Sadie's opinion had mattered to the Detective; and now, as he stared at Mrs. Klein's emotionless profile, he was reminded again of his wife. How often he had tried to convince her; how often he had tried to have her openly affirm his life, his career, and she, too, would deny him victory with the same silent elusiveness: losing every argument but never submitting; letting him talk on but never agreeing, just sitting there quietly in her passive, feminine indomitability. And he sees her now: the high cheeks, the blank stare, the black eyes averted and brushing him out, now and forever brushing him out; the impenetrable veil of her physical silence protecting some secret self which she had always denied him, that self untouched—by him, by any-

146

one . . . or was there someone? The *letters*. The Detective rubbed his legs and turned slightly in his chair toward the gray spray of sky, its spiraling gulls.

"You'd be surprised," he started to say. His voice seemed far away from him and small, as if a muted cry for help from beyond the glass, from that opposite world. "You'd be surprised what can be deduced from just a few facts."

There was no reply; silent, they waited, trapped in their separate worlds—Mrs. Klein hidden behind a lifeless exterior, all emotions withdrawn; the Detective slumped in his chair and drained of will. The mobile spun above them, a chaotic clockwork of twisting wire and speeding propellers, a manic unwinding of a hundred separate time frames all at once, while outside the room, the ocean, caught in its tide, and the sky, rotating through the filtered sunlight, changed in degrees too immense and gradual to be discerned.

"You believe," Mrs. Klein finally said, "you *believe* it's murder, but can you be sure?" She nodded to herself. "Yes, how can you be sure? It might be an accident, or a suicide, or even a little of them all. Yes, that's right, a little of them all, 33.33 percent of each. Perhaps all murders are accidents . . . and suicides, too. Perhaps each murder victim is, to a degree, a co-conspirator, an accomplice in his own death. A man walks the city streets late at night and is killed by a thief, and who's to say—does he himself even know—if he chose to walk those streets because he secretly wished it to happen? And how many times, at the last crucial moment, have people hesitated to rescue themselves from some accidental or murderous danger—isn't that suicide, too?"

"There's the law," the Detective said.

"Oh yes, the law. We believe in the law, don't we? First degree and second degree; felony and misdemeanor; murder,

147

suicide, and accidental death. The coroner's inquest. The declaration. But tell me this—does the law ever say, 'We don't know; it's a mystery and we simply don't know'? Not our law. We can't abide an unsolved mystery, can we? We don't believe in it so we make a declaration anyway: first degree or second degree; murder, suicide, or accident. But does the declaration make it so? Can every death be summed up by just one of three words? Does legal terminology, a court's declaration, tell you what actually happened—ever? Is it ever equal to the event itself?"

The Detective said nothing, but he sympathized with the idea, understood it implicitly—that organic quality, the formal beauty he found in every crime, a wholeness that could not be defined, only sensed viscerally. He had always tried to sketch that organism, that almost living form that was the crime, a form which, in some amoral way, he could appreciate aesthetically. The law, though, devoured subtlety, his complex sketch, his solution, with its ambiguities and shadings, with its own formal beauty, inevitably reduced into crude categories of guilt or innocence. There had been times when he had resented it, this profaning of his art; times when he would have agreed with Mrs. Klein's argument—but he wasn't about to admit that now. Not while still trying to solve the case, not while she mocked his lifelong profession.

"For example," Mrs. Klein said, "what if . . . what if the body that Dexter saw when he saw what he saw, the body we have tentatively identified as Andrew Klein, what if its fall were the result of not one of the possibilities, but all three? What if the body . . ."

"Mr. Klein?" the Detective suggested.

"All right. What if Mr. Klein were to a degree, but only to a degree, a participant in his own demise? Let's assume . . .

yes, let's assume that at the time under question, about five o'clock yesterday evening, Mr. Andrew Klein, sitting in his living room, was suddenly struck by the notion that he'd like to take a walk. And who can say why? Perhaps his legs were stiff; perhaps he felt too warm in the living room or wished to watch the sea birds more closely, a particularly passionate hobby of his; perhaps he had a difficult problem to consider and needed to walk it out. Or perhaps it was just a whim, nothing more than the need to do something, anything, and with the cove before him, a walk was the first thing to come to mind. It could have been any of those reasons or a combination of some or all of them, or something else entirely, and very probably Mr. Klein himself couldn't say for sure. Perhaps it was simply an accident that he should have decided to take a walk, but regardless of our ignorance of his exact motivation, let's assume that Andrew Klein did decide to take that walk. And let's further assume that he took someone along with him, someone close to him, someone who understood him as well as, and perhaps better than, he understood himself."

"His wife perhaps?" the Detective said.

He watched her closely now, sensed a change in her manner—an uneasiness, a tension—the first step perhaps on the road to confession. It was true, he well knew, what they said about criminals wanting to confess; lying by its very nature created a state of anxiety that begged for release. The interrogator, then, was merely guide, midwife, to a natural event; his job at all times to offer up peace of mind in exchange for the truth: the detective as priest.

Mrs. Klein stared at him. "Perhaps," she said. "Perhaps it was his wife."

"Let's assume that it was, shall we?"

149

She hesitated, tugging nervously on the border of her fisherman's sweater. "All right," she finally said. "For the sake of the detective, we will assume that it was his wife . . . Mr. and Mrs. Klein strolling along the walkway of their dream house in Maine, their country retreat, chatting about this and about that as they approached the promontory point overlooking the cove. Who can say what a Nobel prize-winning physicist and his medieval historian wife would talk about on such a walk on such a day? The weather, perhaps? The Uncertainty Principle? The death of the American novel?" She stood up and turned her back to him, facing the cove. "Divorce, perhaps?"

The Detective twisted in his chair, struggling to get a view of her face; every nuance was crucial now, every subtle facial expression could qualify the meaning of her words. But she rotated away from him and hid herself until the moment had passed.

"Just a middle-aged couple strolling along the edge of the cove's cliff, their cove, their cliff; they are silly enough to think that they own them. Just a middle-aged couple chatting about this and about that. It's a January day in Maine, a cold and windy day as all January days in Maine are; there's a blustery wind, fickle, now pushing, now pulling, a challenge to their balance as they walk along the cliff's edge, ernes rising from within the cove helplessly, inevitably, like air trapped in water. A blustery January day in Maine, a middle-aged couple, a promontory point rimmed by a walkway and its railing—do you get the picture?"

The Detective momentarily glanced out through the glass wall, then turned back to Mrs. Klein. "Yes," he said.

"All right, then. Mr. and Mrs. Klein are standing at the promontory point within the walkway's cul-de-sac, leaning

150

right against the railing there, a low railing really, waist high so that it doesn't obstruct the view. And then it happens, the provocation: a gust of wind perhaps, a slip of the foot, some accidental agent; the precipitator, pushing them into this moment, pushing him against the railing and over it, Andrew Klein dangling for an instant on a fulcrum, back arched over the railing, hands cast into the air, balanced, time suspended . . ."

"And Mrs. Klein?"

"And Mrs. Klein facing him, watching him, this man, her husband, her . . . her accomplice, this man she knows better than he knows himself, this man balanced for an instant between the solid ground and the distant ocean, between life and death. And perhaps, just perhaps, she sees in his eyes a plea; not the plea we take for granted, but its opposite, a plea to be left alone, a plea to let this accident happen, a sign that he wishes it to happen, has always wished but never had the courage on his own. She sees this conjectured plea, Mrs. Klein does, and because she knows him better than he knows himself, knows that he wants, has always wanted, this accident to happen, because she is his accomplice in all things in spite of herself, she lets him drop—like the ernes in reverse, she lets him drop, helplessly, inevitably away from her and into the ocean. And what is that? Not legally but really, not in court but in life—an accident? a suicide? a murder?"

Her voice died away as if it, too, were falling into the cove, and turning toward the ocean as it disappeared into silence, she stared into the distance, arms folded, the fisherman's wife keeping her anxious vigil again.

"Perhaps," the Detective said, "just perhaps in this moment we're talking about, Mrs. Klein sees a different plea in her husband's eyes; perhaps she does see the plea we take for granted: the plea for life. And perhaps as she sees this plea, she realizes suddenly that *she* wants, that *she* has always wanted this accident to take place, and realizing this, she lets him fall. A possibility, is it not?"

"Yes," she said softly, still staring toward the cove. "Yes, a possibility."

"And perhaps she not only lets him fall. Perhaps in that moment of realization that she wants, has always wanted, this accident to take place, perhaps she decides to help it take place. Perhaps she disturbs the balance, tips the fulcrum, helps the accident along . . ."

Mrs. Klein turned toward him, her eyes, though, directed above and beyond him, preternaturally still. "Perhaps," she said in a whisper.

The Detective studied her, oblivious to everything but her face, to everything but the case which had distilled itself into this face in this moment—his detective's instinct which carried him now, which controlled him, which became him in this moment, sensing the pressure point, her need to confess.

"Did she, Mrs. Klein?" the Detective asked gently. "Did Mrs. Klein push her husband off the cliff?"

He waited, watching her silently as she dropped her gaze gradually, lowering her line of vision to the chair where he sat: a slow focusing, a curious stare, as though she had just noticed his presence there. Her skin was ghost-white, her hands at her sides; her fingers pinched the nap of her skirt.

"Do you know about Descartes?" she said. "Shall I tell you about Descartes? Shall I give you the lecture, a lesson in history from the medieval scholar?"

"Descartes?"

"Did you know that a historian is a detective too, that a historian seeks something definite too, that just like you I'm in the business of reconstructing crime, the crime of our past? I do that. I collect evidence; sift through the clues, the artifacts; examine motives, relationships, culpability—yes, culpability, too. And there's where we differ, you and I, Andy and I, because I assign blame. It's a historian's most sacred duty, even if only a feedback mechanism for the generations to come, even if it's just a corrective adjustment for the social gyroscope. I assign blame, declare it aloud. Descartes, I say, Descartes: guilty as charged."

"What are you talking about?"

"How could it happen, I ask myself? How could such shortsightedness exist, such self-delusion? The man was a Catholic, a religious man, schooled by Jesuits. His Catholicism mattered to him; they say that as an adult he always asked himself how the Jesuits at La Flèche would receive his work. He refused to see it, though; he refused to admit to it; became indignant at the mention of it. It's just hypothetical, he would say, my work is hypothetical; it isn't necessarily applicable. My work is theoretical, so it can't be a threat. And because he could say that to himself, because he could fool himself with that rationalization, he kept on with his work. This Catholic, this religious man, kept right on destroying the very world he relied on, the very beliefs which gave him comfort and purpose. He turned heaven into a clockwork; he turned God into an idea; he robbed them of meaning; he robbed them of mystery. Descartes killed for all those who came after him what he himself valued most. He was the true end of the Middle Ages; he was the real father of the Modern Age: the first man who could destroy his own world and call it theoretical.

"Are you with me so far? Has my fellow detective kept up with me? Because I'm going to leave you behind now; I'm

153

going to make the leap of faith. I'm going to take up the historian's prerogative and say: guilty, Descartes, guilty as charged."

"Guilty of what?"

"Murder, fellow detective. Descartes killed God."

Mrs. Klein paced in front of the Detective, an absent-minded, irregular path across the thick orange rug; he focused on her face, tried to concentrate and force the connections, but nothing made sense. The feeling, though, was still there, the instinct of the detective, the belief that this was all part of the confession, a need to reduce tension, a gradual, perhaps allegorical revelation of her involvement—if only he could decipher it.

"What are we talking about, Mrs. Klein?"

"The motive, of course. We're talking about the motive for the murder . . ." She paused, a wan and bitter smile flickering across her features. "I mean, of course, the *hypothetical* murder of Andrew Klein."

"And what would that motive be?"

"Revenge. Revenge for the death of God."

"You mean to say that Mrs. Klein killed Mr. Klein because Mr. Klein killed God?"

"Let's say that he was an accomplice in the death of God. It's a possibility, isn't it?"

The Detective shook his head.

"You don't believe it?"

"I believe that Mrs. Klein believes it, but . . ."

"But it's subjective, is that it? It's not the objective truth? It's not what the detective sees when he sees what he sees? Of course not. How stupid of me even to suggest it. The detective, a son of Descartes in a manner of speaking, doesn't believe in God alive *or* dead, does he?"

154

"Not as a motive for murder, he doesn't."

"No, no—of course not. We'll have to try something different then, won't we?" She paced silently for a moment, her
face a caricature of concentration, mimed sarcasm; then, as if
inspired suddenly, she turned to him. "Has the detective ever
been in love? Has he ever been married?"

The Detective hesitated, shades of his earlier suspicion
reappearing, his distrust of her, his reluctance to be exposed
personally. But it was much too late to worry about involvement; he had already lost his professional distance, and, too,
he still believed they were nearing an answer, that just beyond
one of these bends in their meandering conversation, the
solution awaited him.

"Yes," he said, "I've been married."

"Good. We'll start from there then; we'll start from the top.
It's always a good idea to start from what you believe in, and
since the detective believes in marriage, marriage it is—the
motive for the murder, the hypothetical murder of Andrew
Klein."

"Marriage is the motive?"

"No, revenge is still the motive, but revenge for the death
of a marriage instead of revenge for the death of God. You do
believe in the death of a marriage, don't you? The detective
can see that, can't he? It is a possibility, is it not?"

The Detective said nothing, felt the conversation turning
again—on him, out of his control, like his leg, like his heart,
like the last two years of his life, a man adrift in a current he
no longer had the strength to resist, a man afraid. And Mrs.
Klein seemed to feed on his weakness as she probed him with
her bulging eyes.

"Yes, I can see that he does; he believes in its possibility.
But let's analyze it, shall we? Let's take the possibility and

155

analyze it for its likelihood, stretching our minds to meet its implications. We need to flesh it out a bit, this motive; we need something a little more specific. An etiology of a murder, a history of causes, if you will. How about . . ." She nodded to herself. "Yes, how about infidelity—infidelity on the part of the victim's wife?"

"Infidelity?" the Detective said; his voice was no longer his, behind the glass again, far away from him.

"Yes, infidelity; adultery; cheating on one's mate. You do believe in it? It is a possibility?"

The white, feminine-fancy stationery, the rubber band, the slanting curls of Sadie's script . . . it is late, night, and spotlit, stage center, the woman sits. I'm keeping a diary, she says. The man nods, accepts, but now and forever the Detective wanders, peering into, peering from, the blurred and darkened corners, the edges of vision, superimposing new transparencies, analyzing possibilities—but who can tell now, who can tell . . . ?

"Yes," Mrs. Klein said, "yes, I can see that he does. The detective believes it's a possibility. However, let's assume a further motive, a motive for the infidelity, a motive for the motive. All causes are external, says Descartes, every cause has a cause. Hypothetical murder is caused by hypothetical infidelity which, in turn, is caused by the hypothetical death of a marriage. Now what is it, I ask myself as a historian, as a detective in a manner of speaking, what is it that caused this hypothetical death of a marriage? What's the cause of the cause of the cause, I ask myself as a believer in the scientific method? Are you with me, Descartes?"

The Detective felt himself nod.

"All right. So how could it happen, how could this marriage, which started out so wonderfully, die? The man was not

156

unkind. The man was loving and considerate in his own way. His marriage mattered to him; it was the bedrock of his life, in fact. His work, however, was changing him, was beginning to obsess him. He refused to see it, though, refused to admit to it; he became indignant at the mention of it. And because he refused to admit to it, he got worse, became more and more obsessed with his work (which was hypothetical to a degree, which was theoretical), and it was killing his marriage, killing what mattered to him most. Can you see that? Are you with me so far? Is that a possibility for the detective—that someone, without knowing it, could kill what mattered to him most?"

"The absent husband," the Detective said softly. He wet his lips. "The empty vessel."

"Yes," Mrs. Klein said. "Absent. Empty."

"Perhaps, perhaps she didn't let him know. Perhaps if he had only been told . . ."

"Perhaps he couldn't be told. Perhaps no matter how hard she tried, he wouldn't admit to it."

They were silent for a moment. Mrs. Klein retreated to her chair, stepping backward, never taking her eyes from the Detective's.

"Yes," she said, "he couldn't be told. He became obsessed with his work and wouldn't admit to it. And there we have the cause, the hypothetical cause of the death of a marriage. But what's the cause of the cause, I ask myself? I do that. I keep asking myself why he became so obsessed with his work—gruesome, cold work, with awful implications. How could he fool himself with those rationalizations? How could he let his work kill what mattered to him most? Can you tell me that, can my fellow detective please come up with the solution to that? . . . Because I can't."

157

"Perhaps," the Detective said; he shook his head. She waited, pinioned him with her protuberant stare, with its sincerity. "Perhaps," he began again, "she never understood. Perhaps if she had become involved herself, if she had had the gift herself . . . those moments when he was completely engaged, those moments when in the middle of a problem, he felt at peace with himself, carried by something bigger than himself, perhaps if she had felt them too?" He faltered. "Perhaps she never understood."

"No," Mrs. Klein said softly, eyes averted, "no, she never understood."

"So she . . . ?" The Detective hesitated, hoping Mrs. Klein would complete the question; but instead, she only prompted him.

"So she?"

"She was . . . unfaithful?"

"Perhaps—it is a possibility, is it not? But you see, that's what *he* never understood. He never admitted to himself that it was a possibility. Oh, he believed in possibilities, all right, but his possibilities were always hypothetical, theoretical. He never in his heart believed that it could actually take place."

There was a pause, a natural lull, this part of the interrogation brought to a close. Helpless, the Detective stared at Mrs. Klein—she knew, she did know something, about the case, about infidelity—and his glance was a plea for her to stop her teasing, to end the ambiguities and tell him something . . . something definite. For a moment, she seemed to relent, her face gone sad, hidden in her hands, rubbing her eyes with her fingertips; but then, recharged, she surfaced quickly, an actress again, exuding energy—merciless.

"And there we have it; Descartes himself couldn't have done better. Our etiology, our history of causes: his obsession with his work led to the death of their marriage which, in

158

turn, led to her infidelity which, in turn, served as the motive for his murder. All hypothetical, of course. All theoretical."

Mrs. Klein rose from her stainless steel chair and stepped toward the wide glass wall to her left. Behind her hung a canvas, the room's largest, riotous with color; beyond her the sky, still uniformly overcast, had darkened gradually into a premature nightfall, the evening smothered by fuliginous shadows that clung like lichens to the mist-topped, brine-soaked rocks. No gulls or terns crossed the sky now and the Coast Guard cutter had disappeared from view. The dull green of the ocean was gone too; all of the cove, the scene of the crime, framed by the shrieking orange of the drapes, had been bled of its color, merging into shades of the approaching night, toward one black frame, impenetrably opaque. The Detective watched Mrs. Klein as she stared at the cove. She seemed trapped to him then, out of place in the room, a creature indigenous to the outside world, this violent seascape he was forced to call home, but which frightened him, over-whelmed him now with its blunt indifference to human forms; a world he had ignored all his life until Sadie had died, leaving him the letters to open his eyes; a world beyond rooms, be-yond measure, baroque with complexity, whose secrets defied his powers of detection, and which, alien and immense, had begun to cloud his mind with alien thoughts. He had tried to hide from those thoughts, their suspicions, their ever expand-ing, spiraling implications, afraid that he would lose himself in their cold immensity, a mote of matter in infinite space. But then Mrs. Klein had appeared, those thoughts, that world given an advocate, a face and voice for their mysteriousness; and, too, with her sarcastic probing, her relentless intrusion into his private self, an instrument of that world's steel-stark justice: its detective.

A world, a woman, he feared; a crime he could not com-

159

prehend; a life he could no longer with confidence justify, although an end, the end, was drawing near. Fact, he told himself, fact: you're dying. It was Mrs. Klein who reminded him.

"It's about five," Mrs. Klein finally said, "wouldn't you say?"

"Yes—about five."

"It's about time, then, wouldn't you say?" She turned to him, her face passionless; a scale-bearer, implacable Justice. "Time to test the hypothesis."

The Detective swallowed, turned away; Sally would be in the kitchen now, his study—down the hall and around the corner—warm and safe. Looking up again, he shrugged his shoulders, shook his head.

"Oh yes you do," Mrs. Klein said. "You know what I mean—you may not want to, but you do. It's time, Descartes, time for the real detective to take over; time to reenact the crime, test the hypothesis. You *do* understand that the time has come?"

Adrift in the current, unable to turn away, he watched her. Freeze-frame the crime, he has said, says, hears himself say over and over, the words in amber, the climax of detection. Freeze-frame the crime; enter its world; reenact, relive the moment of its occurrence—but if the crime's your life, when the crime's your life . . . ? The Detective turned toward the cove, an alien world darkening: the scene of the crime, the death of Mr. Klein, or just another seaside postcard setting?

"It's a little before five," she said again. "It's time," he heard her say to him.

He didn't move, the mobile spinning above him, the sun—hidden somewhere behind the house, the clouds—dropping faster now, light fading, sight fading. He had thought himself a good husband, a good father . . . The Detective felt a hand tugging gently on his sleeve. Mrs. Klein bent over him; seemed, he thought to whisper to him, a voice from beyond the glass: "I'll help you, Descartes. I'll be your accomplice."

The Detective stood, felt himself stand, silently led to the corner of the room; a slow procession, priestess and penitent, seeress and initiative, seekers after truth in a ritual reenactment—detectives, too, in a manner of speaking. There, at the brink, the oblique angle where glass and plaster met, Mrs. Klein deserted him, slipping behind a strand of drapery, the Detective alone again and staring out . . . at the scene of the crime, the wormwood wilderness of his enforced retirement, this dimmed Maine coast. He reached out, touched the glass, tested its illusions, the cool hard sheen of its sentinel surface, his own image, a wraithlike visage, cast back at him—"pass no further!" Always stopped; always between the see-er and the seen, this cruel exclusion, a glass partition; this permanent exile, the limits of knowledge: Moses, the old man, brought to the top of the mountain and shown where he can never go; Moses, forever dying in the land of Moab, on the other side of what he wished to know. But then, against his skin, the breath of the wilderness, a cold wind penetrating; the pulse of the surf, like the hushed promise of the burning bush, drawing him forward; the drapes thrown open; and there, in the corner, the Red Sea miraculously parting: a door.

The Detective passes through.

A promontory point on the northern coast of Maine. Its rock worn smooth, washed by wind and rain, perpetually damp—always the salt spray, always the fog rolling off the

North Atlantic and condensing on its abraded, undulating face. Daylight asphyxiates; no sun, no stars, no moon, a time when all things become their shadows, when ernes turn invisible and, bodiless, screech from within the cove, a resonating cry muted by the rhythmic rush of the tide, a water-soaked echo. A metallic walkway, raffish orange, arrives at the point from two directions, merges into a cul-de-sac, a low-railed rim around the promontory's edge; and there, sealed in by the fetid ceiling of a sky, framed by the railing and by time, the couple stand face to face. A man, a woman, a promontory point, a moment. The North Atlantic—white-capped, rock-torn—five hundred feet below.

Fact: now and forever it is January.

A man and a woman in a moment. Living, relived, they stand stage center, spotlit by the Detective's eye as he peers into, peers from, the blurred and darkened corners of the crime. Note how the man is propped against the railing; note the arms cast into the air, struggling for balance; note the arched back, the bowed thighs, the heels raised from the ground, toes begging for a hold. Note the face, try to focus on the face—its desperation or surprise, mouth dropping and eyes gone wide, yet focused on the other face. Yes, note the man's face, an expression there, a message, silent because words take time, a plea, but which plea: to live? to die? Note the woman, how she faces the man, close, so close, an arm's length away. Note how their positions balance, how she mimics him in reverse, her shoulders pulled back, arms drawn to her side—a flinch perhaps, a reflex, the body's wisdom beating time? And the face, her face, is there a message there too, a plea? a denial? Note the scene, its formal beauty, its unity, the organic quality appreciated by the aesthetician's eye, and then sketched by him, entitled: "The Fall?" "The Crime?"

A man and a woman in a moment. But there is no title, there is no meaning without movement—and no movement without meaning. In the cove, tide-tossed, Dexter waits, not knowing that he waits; in the bedroom, Sadie waits, pen in hand, not knowing that she waits. For the new scene. The new moment. For another miracle, another door to the world beyond.

It happens; now and forever it happens, one moment into the next, one frame into the other, movement and meaning. She reaches, has reached, is always reaching, her hand on his chest; frozen there at the fulcrum, the critical moment, a time when the world demands an accomplice—everything possible still. In the cove, Dexter waits; in the kitchen, Sally waits, always waiting. Somewhere below a lone gull cries and, time suspended, echoes again and again its crying, waiting for the sound to die, as her hand rests on his chest: to push or to pull? to save or to kill?

The Detective peers into, peers from, the blurred and darkened corners. Note the face, her face, fate's accomplice; the sketch is incomplete, the solution elusive, without understanding that face. But there is only one angle of vision, one point in time and space that can provide the solution. Truth always a risk, to know or not to know—only he can decide.

It happens; now and forever it happens, one frame into another; he too becomes fate's accomplice, taking a step into the world beyond. The Detective becomes, has become, is always becoming a man in a moment, a man at a railing, back arched, arms cast into the air, heels raised from the ground, toes begging for a hold—the North Atlantic, rock-torn, five hundred feet below. The Detective becomes this man in this moment, the man at the fulcrum, his wife's hand on his chest, and who can say, does he himself even know for sure, which

163

plea is in his own eyes? But note the face now, her face in this moment, the key to the solution—the protuberant eyes, the pride smoldering in silence. Is the jittery search over? Is the dream at its climax? Have all the accusing glances been merged into one?

A man, a woman, a promontory point, a moment. Helplessly, Descartes awaits the judgment of history; passively Moses, the sentence of God. Helplessly, passively, with her hand on his chest, the truth-seeker, the detective, awaits the solution; the absent husband, the declaration: to be pushed or to be pulled? affirmation at last or guilty as charged?

But does it happen—now or ever? objectively or in a manner of speaking? And who can say, does she herself even know for sure, the declaration, the final answer? No, she fails him; no longer an accomplice, she withdraws her hand; no longer his inspiration, she withdraws into mystery, into movement whose meaning can never be spoken, whose essence can never be frozen. No, the moment fails him; hypothetical, it is a possibility never to be born. And answerless, he waits; judgment ever suspended, he waits, while somewhere below them, the gull's cry dies and dissolves within the wash of the tide.

They sat silently in the living room before the glass wall. Brine dampened the Detective's forehead and salted his lips, and he dabbed at it slowly with his handkerchief as he emitted a series of involuntary sighs. His heart wasn't racing, the pain in his leg bearable, but weighed down by an exhaustion so complete that even gravity seemed palpable, sucking at every muscle and drawing him down into death, he suddenly threw back his head and stretched for air, gasped like a whale at the surface, trying to inflate himself with life. Mrs. Klein sat close to him, her face blood-drained and expressionless, her short gray hair, wet along its edges, hanging in water-darkened points across her forehead like a crown of thorns. She seemed to shrink before him, a change from menacing interrogator to plausible widow, and attempting to pace his recovery with hers, the Detective watched her closely, waiting for signs. But ever a mystery, she hid from him, hid behind the glass shell of her excluding silences, and unable to break through, too tired to speak, to think, he waited as night obscured the cove and darkened the room.

She shivered; the Detective watched her shiver, a sudden disruptive shuddering which caught him by surprise, her arms and legs twitching, chest shaking. Amazed, he thought: "Her feet barely touch the ground." She was motionless for a moment, as if in that one violent exorcism, she had expelled some core of coldness she had absorbed from the out-of-doors; but then, the shaking began again, her hands thrown up to her face, her fingers quaking, muffling sounds—were those sobs he heard?

The Detective fought to stand, struggling out of his chair, out of his bone-drenched exhaustion and onto his feet, all motion a compromise now between speed and pain. The room reeled as the weight of his body shifted to his feet, became an extension of its own decor—the swirling paintings and spinning mobile—until the Detective steadied himself, his hand grasping the arm of the chair. Limping, he slowly crossed the room and stood beside her, staring down at her sobbing body. At a loss for a moment, indecisive, his hand fumbled like a clumsy lover's until, finally, it found its object, settling softly on the back of her head. There, in some lullaby of comfort, of gentle caring, he caressed her hair.

"It's all right," he said.

He waited there above her, a watchful father, until her

crying had spent itself and her shuddering had receded to a slumped, still calm. Then, when she reached up and softly touched his hand—an expression of gratitude, a sign of recovery—he returned to his chair and sat down again. They remained there in their chairs, in their silence, in the dark, the room's meager light scattered around them like the firefly memories of an old man's childhood. He could just barely discern her face across from him; no longer blank or bitterly ironic, it mourned now—a solemn, passive grief, a glowing ember of pain, slow-burning and eternal. There was a purity to her suffering, a depth beyond feeling, a breadth beyond personality which awed the Detective, made him feel responsible, as though he were sole witness to a sacred ritual. He needed no words from her now; the power of her grief was eloquence enough, and he wished only to remain there forever, a quiet mirror to her sad surrender.

But then, the sound of tires biting into gravel, of car doors slamming and approaching voices, drew him out of that calm, reminding him that the Chief would be returning any moment, reminding him that he had a case before him, a case still unsolved—he had been alone with Mrs. Klein for over three hours and still didn't know if there had been a crime. Pride, fear of failure, allegiance to the old self-image, panicked him; he had to have something for them, something definite. And so, ashamed of himself but helpless to act upon it, he heard himself violate their perfect silence.

"Mrs. Klein?"

She turned toward him. Although only five feet away, she seemed removed from him, as distant as death from life; beyond the glass again, as if she had never returned. She watched him, waited.

"Did you . . . ?" he started to say, but suddenly incapable

166

of completing the question, of profaning her mourning, he stopped. He knew what he should ask, what a detective should want to know, but his time with her nearly over, he sensed that there was another, more important and personal question to ask, one that only Mrs. Klein could answer for him, if he just knew how to phrase it. Desperate, he struggled after it, a form for his need, words slipping through his fingers, though, failing him. "Did you . . . ?" he began again, but again he faltered; his hands, pleading with her, kneaded the air.

Mrs. Klein nodded. The Detective watched her nod to him and felt relief—teammates, they understood each other; teammates, they completed each other; she would give him what he needed to know.

"I loved him," Mrs. Klein said.

The Detective leaned forward; her voice, soft, receding, drew him toward her, and he paused in expectation as she held her breath. She closed her eyes, and her face, radiant with pain, seemed to float before him, to drift on the exhalation of her whispered answer.

"I love him."

The Detective sat motionless and silent, a dumb and stunned supplicant before the priestess, weighing her oracle, unsure of its meaning. Footsteps outside the room finally broke the spell, twisting him in his chair; her voice, though, followed him there, refusing to let him go.

"I'll tell you," she said.

He turned back to her. She nodded to herself, opening her eyes.

"If you must, if you must know, come back to me—I'll tell you then. But for now, I can only give you this: whatever happened, it was for the best."

167

The Detective stared at her, trying to freeze-frame the face, to draw it out of the darkness and fixate on it, extracting from it the meaning of her words—a friend's promise or the last obfuscation of a desperate defense? Incredibly, he thought he saw a shade of a smile appear there, not quite mockery and certainly not joy, something of sadness endured, of survival, but he couldn't be sure: there was too little light, too little time to consider, the door creaking open, a surprised silence following the first steps in.

"Hello?" the Chief finally called out into the darkened room.

They didn't answer; the Detective refused even to turn in his seat, his eyes locked on hers. The smile dissolved. He saw her nod to him once (the last line of her message or just another meaningless gesture?) before she disappeared into the glare of the room's struck lights. And then, by the time his eyes had recovered, he found a different woman sitting before him, the one he sought withdrawn again, her face as cold and featureless as glass.

"There you are," the Chief said as he walked toward them, Officer Truax trailing behind. Mrs. Klein immediately rose from her chair and, without a word, left the room. The Chief let her go, waiting until she had disappeared behind a closed door before sitting in her chair. There, he unzipped his official coat and placed his hat on his knee. He turned toward the Detective.

"For a moment there I was afraid I'd lost two more people."

"You haven't found him yet?"

"I haven't; the city cops where he teaches haven't; the Coast Guard hasn't. And that leads us right back here to you."

The Detective ignored the implied question, instead staring

168

at the door where Mrs. Klein had stood just moments before. "She's a strange woman," he said.

"Can't disagree with you on that. And to be honest with you, it's comforting to hear someone else say it. After a full morning of interrogating her, I was beginning to wonder if *I* wasn't a little strange. She's a challenge, all right." The Chief paused, struggling to be polite, to maintain his patient composure. "Well?" he finally asked.

The Detective shrugged.

"Come up empty-handed?" Officer Truax said; standing beside the Chief, he smiled sarcastically.

"I don't know."

"He don't know," Truax said to the Chief.

"I got ears, Truax." The Chief leaned forward. "You don't sound too sure about that," he said to the Detective. "You sound like you just might have something."

The Detective was silent; he sensed suddenly the widening gap between already divergent loyalties, afraid then of betraying either side. He looked to the glass wall for a moment, but it was full night now and the cove, the ocean, the sky were nearly indistinguishable.

"I don't know. I'll have to think about it."

"Yes," the Chief said; he looked toward the ceiling. "Yes, why don't you do that. Tried it myself this afternoon—sat alone and tried to sort out the facts, to get some distance on it. Didn't have much luck, frankly, but maybe you'll do better. Just give me a call if you come up with anything."

"I'll do that."

The Chief stood. "I had to chase Charlie Wriggins away from here. He was parked down the road, waiting to ambush you for the inside scoop, killing himself from carbon monoxide poisoning. I figured you'd want to avoid him for

169

awhile anyway; he can be a real pain in the neck when he gets like this. I'll have Truax here drop you off at your home."

The Detective rose slowly; he accepted the Chief's hand and shook it.

"I appreciate it," the Chief said, "I appreciate you coming over here and taking a shot at it."

The Detective nodded; felt again the camaraderie, the bond of common work. You're a good man, he wanted to say; you're one of the good ones, one of the professionals. A good man not to have acknowledged my failure, to have remained a gentleman in spite of your job—not many do; Sadie had been right about that. But he didn't say it; instead, he reached out with his second hand and grasped the Chief's more firmly. Wavering from fatigue after a moment, though, he fumbled for support.

"Are you all right?" the Chief said. "Do you want to lie down for a few minutes?"

The Detective steadied himself, keeping his eyes off the mobile's spinning blades, its clockwork universe machinations. "No, no, I'm okay—but I better get home. My daughter will have supper waiting for me."

3

The Detective sat in his study's easy chair, his eyes closed, his feet resting on the cracked leather ottoman, time suspended, body suspended; only the wave of heat pressing against his cheek from the fireplace beside him and the warmth radiating from the food in his belly reminded him that he was alive, a reminder as casual and pleasant as the sound of rain against a roof at night, or the first shovel's scraping on a snow-bound morning. The best times in an old man's life were when, free of pain, he could forget his body—times of rest, of slow recollection. The old rested well; they practiced their dying. Perhaps it won't be so terrible, after all, the Detective thought; but then, suddenly frightened, irrational: perhaps it's happening now. The Detective stirred his legs; they talked back to him with their pain, their angry exhaustion, telling him that he was alive. For now, he thought, for this moment, one more night. And what would it be like? A serene, sleepy withdrawal from consciousness like a wave from the shore? Or painful, an awful wrenching, something torn from your chest, from your mind; a separation, you from your life? You die alone. An old man was forced to suffer too many separations as it was, a parade of goodbyes, subtractions of the vital stuff—people he loved, a way of life. The Detective thought of Sadie then, ached for her, and not just her words or the sight of her, and not even her touch in the night, but a knowledge beyond the senses, a feeling he had had when lying beside her, a wordless and secure belief in her life. This much we owe each other, the Detective thought, the assurance that someone will be beside you, a human hand for your head when you're crying, dying . . . He shouldn't have left Mrs. Klein alone.

From the next room, the Detective heard his granddaughter Nan's laughter, girlish still, flirting with his consciousness, obscured by the crackling of burst wood fiber and the hot exhale of the fire. How reassuring that laughter was, reminding him of how Sadie had smiled at Sally's childhood laughter, and of how he had smiled at the two of them, his family frame-frozen in a happy moment. Etiology, Mrs. Klein had called it, the cause of the cause: her laughter caused her smile caused his smile, a case history for the cure to his loneliness—not hypothetical, but simply gone. Did Mrs.

171

Klein have children and grandchildren, he wondered, or was her husband all that she had? And how could that ever be for the best—to be deserted on that rock overlooking the ocean, that desolate point? The city, though, was not much better, the Detective suddenly remembered. During those first few weeks after the funeral, there were a million hands to stroke his head, but no one had touched him. Perhaps no one could.

Nan's laughter disappeared now, and the Detective struggled to find it; tried to will its existence out of the busy respiration of the fire; pleaded to hear it, a lifeline to the world beyond his solipsistic study, beyond his time. They had sneaked Nan into the hospital the week before Sadie had died, he remembered. Sadie herself had begged them to break the rules, asking time and time again until, guilt-ridden, they were forced to give in. Ten years old then, Nan had been unselfconscious and energetic, bouncing around the room and from subject to subject, first offering to recite a poem she had learned, but then forgetting about it, caught up in relating the outrage of a schoolgirl betrayal. How Sadie had smiled at Nan that day, radiant, content for the first time since she had been told there could be no cure, a smile miraculously defying her pain and the stuporous drugging to kill it. The Detective had been jealous of his own granddaughter then, jealous of her effortless ability to bring happiness to Sadie, happiness that should have been his to give.

But now as he strained to hear Nan's laughter once again, as *he* pleaded for her presence in the room, the Detective felt that jealousy leave him. Now, for the first time, he sensed fully what Nan had given Sadie that day a week before her death; understood the importance of having someone beside you in time as well as in space—no emptiness to touch you; everywhere, in every direction, every dimension, past and

172

future too, a familiar loving face, part of yourself, to greet you. Now at the edge himself, near the end himself, he could no longer rue any happiness for anyone, any escape from loneliness, and certainly not for Sadie, the one he cared about most, the one he cared about even now, as if she were still alive, a form stirring in his mind, begging for comfort. Too late. He couldn't help her now; nor she, him.

The Detective suddenly remembered the letters. The pure thought, unsuppressed; the clarified image projected before him: the white, feminine-fancy stationery, the rubber band, two lines of Sadie's script. And he waited—for the racing heart, for his body, his thoughts to leap out of rhythm, for the uncontrolled anger and jealousy, the paralyzing fear. But they never came, in their place a sadness so profound, so all-consuming, that he was past crying; and in his mind's eye, he saw Mrs. Klein again, her passive grief as they had sat alone in her living room, but this time she was *his* mirror, the image of *his* lonely survival. The letters, their physical existence, their presence in the desk drawer beside him; the letters, his soul's metronome, his every dream's question, the one sure key to his unsolved case. The letters. Now that he could remain calm in the face of them, now that he could consider them without his body erupting, they seemed to fill him up with the simple fact of their existence, seemed the very word and substance of the sadness he felt, and an accusation in themselves.

Before, and until now, that accusation had always been directed at Sadie, a flush of incredulous anger at her potential betrayal. But now that he could consider the letters more passively, analyzing them the way a detective should, he went one step further, searched for the cause of the cause, and began to shift the blame onto himself. The Detective had failed his wife, failed to make her happy—as with Nan in the

173

hospital, when in need, Sadie had turned to someone else. The Detective couldn't bear that; even now he wondered if he could bear the realization that she had been forced to go outside of him for comfort, that he hadn't been enough. And helpless, he saw her once again lying on her death bed: Sadie, his Sadie, her flesh stripped and eroded by a pain so insistent that it couldn't be dismissed—no false hopes, no lasting relief—the finality of its meaning undeniable. And he wondered about the other, earlier pains, the ones he might have eased, the aches and hurts hidden behind her silent, uncomplaining face, her plea-less pride. Too late now. He had failed to soothe those more subtle pains when it had been possible; he hadn't even been aware of their existence, hiding them from himself. If only he had known, if only he had forced himself to see, if only he had been aware when he could have made a difference . . . if only he could comfort her now, to make her happy now would bring him peace.

He couldn't bear it; even now the Detective couldn't bear the thought of her in pain: Sadie on her death bed; Sadie's emaciated face; Sadie's eyes, frightened, searching his for peace. But there was no comfort for an agony so real, so unhypothetical—only an end. He couldn't help her, not now, not then; able only to watch, a dumb witness to the death of his happiness. It was painless in the end, the doctor had told him; it was painless in the end, the doctor had tried to console. Painless for whom, the Detective had wanted to scream as he watched Sally sob in her husband's arms, Nan clinging to her coat. I died, I died then, too, he had told himelf time and time again; but he knew now that it wasn't true. You die alone.

The Detective heard the phone ringing in the hallway. He opened his eyes, startled by its sound, an alarm retrieving him to another world, the present tense, the here and now. The call was for him, he suddenly knew with clairvoyant surety, Charlie Wriggins or the Chief; either way an inquiry into the case, pressure to decide whose side he would take. If you must, if you must know, Mrs. Klein had told him, come back. But would she really tell him? First degree or second degree; murder, suicide, or accidental death, they weren't the language of her version of the truth, but it was the only language that Charlie Wriggins and the Chief—that the law—could accept. The law, he had served it all his life; could he turn his back on it now by ignoring a solution? could he betray his allegiance to the lifelong cause, to his own self-image? The Detective wondered if the old ideas mattered to him anymore. People, though, he knew, did matter; loyalty to a man meant more than allegiance to an idea, and he felt bound to the Chief. To ignore the possibility of an answer was to betray the Chief— not literally, not legally perhaps, but in fact; there was no escaping that. Just as there was no escaping the bond he felt to Mrs. Klein, the marriage of their common grief, his desire, his need to comfort and protect.

The Detective heard his daughter's footsteps in the hall and then (he imagined them in his mind just before they occurred) three sharp knocks on his study door. He closed his eyes when, after a pause, the door swung open.

"Dad," he heard Sally call softly.

He didn't move; he breathed through his nose; his belly rose and fell slowly as he sensed her drawing closer.

"Dad," she said softly, "it's for you."

The Detective sat motionless, time suspended, body suspended; he didn't need to open his eyes to see his daughter now. They were so close, so interdependent, that he knew her face better than he knew his own: the pinched concern, the constant conflict between fear and caring; always the struggle to do the right thing, features flexed in perpetual moral crisis.

She was at that age when one thought one ran the world, when one assumed responsibility for it, a middle-aged martyrdom. It seemed so silly, so sad to him now, the Sea Gull Sallys striving to save us all, and for an instant he thought he might sit up and tell her: "Leave it alone, Sally; it will happen on its own." But time suspended, body suspended, he didn't move; knew at last that he wouldn't, couldn't tell her. That was what old age was for—you had to feel it in your bones before you could believe that it was true.

The room seemed so calm, his body so painless and peaceful, that the Detective felt as if he could wait there forever with his breath held. Only the fire was impatient, busily consuming itself, a hushed but relentless rustling beside him. He knew that his daughter still hovered above him, indecisive and concerned, and he knew too, in another feat of detection, that she would call out to him one more time—out of guilt for having hung up earlier in the afternoon, out of concern for his, her father's feelings; because she cared about him, because despite her worrying and her need to maintain control, she would do what she thought would make him happy as best she could. And when she did that, when she leaned closer and once again called softly just above the steady pant of the fire, "Dad," he wanted to reach up and hug her for her effort. She tried so hard, her struggling ascent out of the pith of her own failures into kindness was so desperately human that he was moved to recognize it, to let her know that he knew. But by the time he could arouse his inert body—raise his head and open his eyes—the study door was closing, her back disappearing behind it.

Too late, again too late to give comfort to his family. The Detective straightened up in his chair and conversed with his body, the language of old age, the paradox of suffering; reminding him that he was, at the same time, both alive and dying; arousing a fear that he would die before Sally would return again, before he could show her how much she mattered to him—a curse-prayer-promise tossed out into the night begging his survival for just that much longer. There seemed no end to this business of living, only to life itself; always a few more facts needed to settle the issue, solve the case. Death seemed to lack resolution; he put it off with these pleas for reprieve because he had too many things to do, a lifetime of loose ends to tie up. At the end, one should be able to gather all of the accomplices in one's life into a single room as at the climax of a murder mystery story, and there resolve one's relationships with them; explain every false lead and missed connection, reveal the alibis and extenuating circumstances; and then, after assigning guilt, bestow and receive forgiveness in an ordered, happy finale. If only he could see Sally just one more time before he died, one more chance to explain his feelings; if only he could have seen his father one more time, held his hand as he was dying; and Sadie, above all Sadie, if only she had told him, if only she had understood . . . My gift, the Detective thought, was detection, a miraculous gift that appeared as if from nowhere, that wasn't even mine except to cherish and protect, that will leave me like a soul when I die, that seems to have deserted me already, the vessel empty, a prelude to the end. Detection was my gift and I wasn't very good at anything else; but I tried, Sadie, I did try, he wanted to tell her. I hope you knew, I hope you felt it somewhere behind the silence I so rarely broke through—how much you mattered, how much I would have sacrificed for you if I had only known how. To ease your suffering, to quiet your pain, I would have absorbed it all myself. I hope you knew, I hope you know that I'd accept, that I'd embrace even this awful loneliness if it brought you peace.

The Detective suddenly remembered Mrs. Klein, felt again

the shaking of her shoulders beneath his hand, heard again the palm-stifled sounds of her crying. And he was reminded of the endless and multiform suffering of all the men and women in his life, pain's many faces: his daughter sobbing in a hospital waiting room, Sadie's searching eyes, the Chief's perplexed exhaustion. Even Dexter's rigid mask couldn't hide from him now the shared anxiety in them all, the quiet, constant fear best expressed by Sally's need to intervene, her lack of faith: *life dies when you close your eyes—better not blink!* He would have reduced them all if he could have, compressed them into the quaking form of Mrs. Klein; and there he would have reached out and touched them, a benediction for the tired and frightened; there he would have told them, all the suffering survivors: "It's all right."

But could he say that to himself? Where was the source of peace in the world for an old man past his time? Could one offer comfort, forgiveness to oneself? There were moments when he had sensed a peace in Mrs. Klein, moments when he had believed she was tapping its secret source, moments when, as she had probed him, he had felt her to be his teacher and guide, possessor of a strange wisdom he had only begun to understand. She seemed then to beckon to him, to bring him closer. But in the end, she had only been human; in the end she had cried like everyone else, lonely like everyone else, just another of pain's many faces, although her suffering and isolation had seemed more perfectly complete, more fully understood—but was that because they were self-induced? I'll tell you, she had promised him at the day's end, two survivors grieving in the dark. Come back and I'll let you know. Would she, though?

The Detective felt buoyant, expanding suddenly with that old sensation of dispossession, of time suspension, that in-

178

stinctual belief preceding the infallible solution—his gift returning. But now, for the first time in his life, the gift frightened him; seemed now to have been infected by his philosophizing, by the uncertainy of those strange thoughts which had afflicted the last years of his life, bringing him not an answer unquestionable, not a solution, but another question in itself. And that question wasn't, would she tell him, but rather, could she? Did even Mrs. Klein know for sure? Would her answer, if she provided one, be anything more than a pro forma gesture to satisfy the law? Would it be anything more than an act of friendship, a reciprocal kindness to the Detective, giving him only what he wanted, what he felt he had to know, rather than the truth? And could he now, after his day alone with her, after those moments at the promontory point, could he himself accept any of the definite answers? Was there ever, the Detective suddenly thought, terrified by the thought, was there ever a solution? Not to satisfy the law, but for him, for her, for any man or woman? Was there ever an etiology, a chain of facts to be relied upon? Could one ever close one's eyes while at the brink, on the edge, and still be sure? I'll tell you, she had said. If you must know, if you must . . .

The Detective rose, felt himself rise, above his chair, above his pain and exhaustion, the accrued erosion of a hard day, a hard life; and carried by his concentration, only the case to be solved on his mind, he walked past the fire to the desk beside him. Bending, one hand propped against the writing top for balance, he opened a drawer and removed a pack of letters, raising them then before his eyes.

A pause then, a lingering sensation—tantalizing, frightening—of proximity in time and space to a conclusion, a crisis. Now unavoidably fate's accomplice, he feared his freedom, the weight of the impending decision, forced complicity in life—he alone to decide. The Detective's mind reeled for a moment, spinning memories of Sadie, a multitude of images from the days of their lives, all the framed scenes, the stored immortalities, the secured niches where she still lived in his mind, and all illuminated it seemed at the same time, an explosion of her being inside him. Sadie as his fiancée, Sadie as his wife, Sadie as a mother, breastfeeding their child, Sadie a thousand different times, tagged by a thousand different titles, and appearing so rapidly that they began to blur in his mind, becoming not one picture, not many pictures, but beyond them all, until he could no longer see her face or hear her voice, but just accept and believe in her life.

A thought occurred to the Detective then, appearing in its entirety as if by magic. Perhaps he had read it somewhere or overheard it in conversation, but having lost the mental tenacity to force the connections, he couldn't recall its source, only the thought itself: "Identity is more than just content." He would leave it to the Sallys, to the new generation of detectives, to chart the etiologies, to trace it back to its origins; he was through with that now. Instead, he held onto the thought, to the feeling it described, to Sadie's presence, so real to him now that he believed her by his side: the reprieve granted at last, a little more life; one last chance to show her that she mattered, to break through the silence, to ease her pain and earn his own peace by it; one last chance to prove that he loved her. His choice now. His freedom to decide.

The Detective stands, has stood, is always standing, a man in a moment, a man in his study, a study middle class in all respects, Victorian Yankee. Its leather easy chair, oxblood red; the slotted cupboard of its roll-top desk; its bookshelves, inset, their contents arranged by subject; its Tiffany reading lamp illuminating the hung emblems of success, Latin-graved plaques and framed newspaper print—all evoke the bourgeois faith in order, in justice: that wild hope-belief in the eventual redress of effort with reward. A flagstone hearth and carved wooden mantel, memento-adorned with a Sherlock Holmes hat and luridly gleaming, fake gold statuettes, frame the fireplace, whose controlled destruction, a slow explosion of heat and light, hypnotizes this old man, this detective. Gravity-bent, he stands there, an arm outstretched, a pack of letters balanced on his palm. Flames, searing yellow against the black-charred brick, leap chaotically beneath his hand.

Fact: he is alone.

A man in a moment, a man in a crisis, the Detective peers into, peers from, the blurred and darkened corners of his life—for sense, for shape, for the sure means to decide, the sure lines. But there is no frame to the frame when you're in it; there is no meaning without movement and no movement without dying. Everything grows tentative, vaporous, murky, his life undefined, its borders stretching beyond the limits of his eyes, his mind. For him, no safe enclosure; just empty space, black infinity, the unknown to hold him.

The Detective stands, has stood, is always standing, a man in this moment, a man at a fire, the letters balanced on his palm, he alone to decide—to forgive, forget? to let the question die? Living, relived, Mrs. Klein waits, hoping as she waits. Living, relived, Sadie waits, hoping as she waits, the unseen silent presence by his side. Helplessly, passively, with his hand on her chest, the murderess, the unfaithful wife, await the declaration, guilt or redemption, while outside the study a girl is heard laughing, and time suspended, is always heard laughing above the coarse, rasping voice of the fire.

But does it happen—now or ever? objectively or in a man-

181

ner of speaking? Can it really come to this: destruction of the evidence? Can it really be a case of "no corpse, no crime"? No, ignorance fails him; now and forever he knows that it fails him, forgetfulness too hypothetical to be born. Forgiveness is not to forget what he can never forget, but is instead to live the question, to suffer and survive it, to know always that he will never know and to accept that. Forgiveness is to sacrifice the old self-image, to deny his gift of detection, is to leave, now and forever, the case unsolved . . . because he loved her. Because he loves her.

The Detective stands, has stood, is always standing. Always a hand on his chest; always poised at the fulcrum, on the cutting edge of paradox where opposites meet: judged and judging, alive and dying in the same moment—suffering. And waiting, always waiting for the miracle, for a reprieve he must believe in from a sentence he must take on faith alone as well. Always a man with the unknown before him; always alone at the end. But in spite of that, it happens; now and forever, he makes it happen; the sufferer, the survivor, he alone decides—becomes fate's accomplice, an accessory to the crime. He leans; he steps; he moves yet closer, daring even to close his eyes. And love spills from his palm, an old man's affirmation, into the purging flames, the purifying ocean, from one moment to the next, from one frame to another, the miracle: life.

In 1980 the Howard Heinz Endowment of Pittsburgh, Pennsylvania, through a grant to the University of Pittsburgh Press, created the Drue Heinz Literature Prize to recognize and encourage the writing of short fiction. The first prize was awarded in 1981 to David Bosworth for The Death of Descartes.